"THERE ISN'T MUCH FOR ME HERE, IS THERE?"

"No family?" Damian asked. "No man?"

"Goodness, no. How would I ever explain myself to one?"

"Why in the world should you?" Damian reached for Lark, raising her chin with a single finger and peering into her eyes. "Any man would be foolish to cast you away merely because of a past, shall we say, 'industrious' nature."

Lark froze, lost in his touch. "Any man?" Her breath caught in her throat.

Impulsively, Lark leapt up on her toes, straining to reach Damian's height. She hoisted herself up and pressed her lips against his, willing, with every fiber of her being, for Damian to respond . . .

Thieves at Heart

ALINA ADAMS

AVON BOOKS ◆ NEW YORK

THIEVES AT HEART is an original publication of Avon Books. This work has never before appeared in book form. This work is a novel. Any similarity to actual persons or events is purely coincidental.

AVON BOOKS
A division of
The Hearst Corporation
1350 Avenue of the Americas
New York, New York 10019

Copyright © 1995 by Alina Sivorinovsky
Published by arrangement with the author
Library of Congress Catalog Card Number: 95-94492
ISBN: 0-380-78293-6

First Avon Books Printing: December 1995

AVON TRADEMARK REG. U.S. PAT. OFF. AND IN OTHER COUNTRIES, MARCA REGISTRADA, HECHO EN U.S.A.

Printed in the U.S.A.

RA 10 9 8 7 6 5 4 3 2 1

1

In the Autumn of 1818, Lord and Lady Raynes threw a small dinner party for the largest diamond in England.

The bauble in question spent the bulk of its evening resting comfortably in a gold band on Lady Raynes' index finger, and, to all appearances, enjoying itself tremendously.

Lord Raynes, whose purchase of the jewel had warranted wildly disparate mentions in both that morning's *London Times* and *Examiner*, took great pleasure in watching the procession of curious visitors coming by to pay their respects to his wife's ring. And, when it looked like the dinner conversation might be beginning to stray from his cleverness in acquiring the coveted treasure, Lord Raynes would remember another highlight of the months he'd spent bargaining for the diamond, and all faces would once again turn with respectful admiration in his direction.

By midnight, even his wife and daughter were starting to grow weary of the oft-repeated, albeit frequently embellished, tale, and Phillipa begged, ''Please, Papa, no more. We are all very well aware of how the story ends.''

Lord Raynes harrumphed, sucking in his cheeks and puffing out both lips to resemble a freshly caught mackerel awaiting its fate on the chopping block, and prepared to treat his daughter to his favorite lecture on The Impertinence of Young People Today, when the butler appeared to announce that there was a very tardy, very wet, young lady at the door, claiming to be delivering a message for Lord and Lady Raynes from the Duchess of Hayley.

Curious, Lady Raynes suggested that the child be brought inside, the presence of a glittering thousand pound ring rendering her unusually generous as she observed that not even a dog or a Frenchman should be forced to remain out of doors on such a miserable, cold, and windy night.

The assembled guests tittered in approval at her humorous little remark, followed by self-mocking cries of, "Oh, my, aren't we just awful?" and then more laughter.

Fortunately, Lady Raynes' charity proved well-founded, when the misplaced miss in question shuffled meekly into the salon and proved herself a girl of good family and breeding with her fine yellow muslin frock, white gloves, and the pattens on her shoes, all of which, despite their presently drenched state, testified to her being a young lady of fine upbringing.

Chestnut colored curls peeked out timidly from beneath her bonnet, framing a round face with tiny, delicate features, and a pair of green eyes, shimmering like bottomless summer lagoons.

She curtsied before Lord and Lady Raynes, and, in a voice barely above a whisper, introduced herself as Miss Lark Talbot, companion and secretary to the Duchess of Hayley. She curtsied again while handing Lord and Lady Raynes the duchess' written regret at being unable to attend their little soiree, and explained that she would have surely arrived sooner if the horse on the first coach she set out in had not taken lame, and stranded her outside of London.

"The duchess preferred to send her response with me, rather than put your lordship and ladyship through the inconvenience of paying for such a negative piece of mail.

She is off to visit her son in India, and has no more need for my secretarial services. However, before she left, the duchess took care to arrange for a temporary position for me at the home of her friend, Lady Stuart. I asked that the cab take me by their home before arriving here, so that I might drop off some of my things, but the Stuart residence appears quite closed up for the season. Not a light burning anywhere. Isn't that most odd?"

"It's not odd at all," Phillipa looked first to her gentleman friend, Damian Moxley, then to her parents for confirmation. "Aren't the Stuarts and their relations visiting Switzerland until at least Boxing Day this year?"

Miss Lark Talbot gasped, one hand jerking up to cover her mouth, and hurriedly mumbled a host of apologies. Her eyes filled with tears. She attempted to wipe them away, but the sodden state of her handkerchief only made things worse.

"What is it, Miss Talbot?" Lady Raynes nervously tugged at the precious ring on her finger, hoping that the girl would not pitch a fit of some sort in the midst of her very meticulously planned dinner party.

"It is nothing, my lady." Miss Talbot shook her head from side to side and stared down at the floor, blushing furiously at the puddle forming underneath the damp hem of her dress.

"Come, come, no one weeps over nothing, child." Lord Raynes, who wished to put an end to this embarrassment as soon as possible so that he might return to his triumphant tale of bargain and bluff, snapped his fingers and demanded, "You had best tell all to us now, and quickly."

Lark tiredly rubbed her eyes and confessed, "It is only that I had depended on this job with the Lord and Lady Stuart for my livelihood in London. You see, I have no other place to go. The Duchess of Hayley swore that she had arranged it all, but, I should have known, her faculties are not what they once were and—"

For the second time that evening, Miss Talbot covered

her mouth guiltily and gasped, "Oh, please forgive me. I did not mean to suggest—she is a fine woman. The finest. It is only that, well, you see, her age . . . Oh, I knew that I should have sent for my own confirmation, I just knew it."

"You have no family in London that might put you up?" Damian Moxley looked away from the hanging damask he'd been contemplating for the past quarter of an hour, and curiously raised his head.

"None, sir. I am afraid that I am all alone in the world."

"Yes. I expected as much."

For a moment, their eyes met. Lark blinked in surprise, wondering why he was staring at her so queerly, his hazel pupils unblinking in their intensity. In spite of herself, Lark shivered. She drew the sopping cape tighter about her shoulders, forcing herself to break their gaze and look away.

"Well, this truly is a mess then, isn't it?" It was hard to tell from Phillipa Raynes' tone whether she meant the homeless girl's situation or the water dripping off her clothes and onto their fine Indian carpet.

"I shan't disturb you any longer." Lark turned towards the door, swallowing hard at the sound of rain and wind smashing against the window-sill. "And I thank you ever so kindly for your generous hospitality towards me."

Lady Raynes snuck a guilty glance at her husband, wondering how it might appear at tea-time gossip the next day if they let it be known that Lord and Lady Raynes, on the same evening as the unveiling of her stunning diamond, had sent a poor, orphan girl unprotected out into the vicious elements.

Wouldn't the radicals at the *Examiner* just trip all over themselves to tell such a tale, painting the Raynes family in the most vile, and wholly undeserved, colors?

"My lord." She turned to her husband. "Was I not saying only this morning how desperately I am in need of a young lady to help with my daily correspondence and other such household tasks?''

''Mama!'' Now it was Phillipa's turn to gasp, as she crossed both arms against her chest and demanded, ''Surely, you are not suggesting that we take this . . . this horribly wet stranger, into our household?''

''But, Phillipa, my darling, she could be a great help to us. After all, what, with the upcoming Season, this house is bound to be inundated with invitations and callers. And, who knows, at the end of it, we might very well find ourselves needing to address an even larger correspondence. Say, invitations of our own, to one sort of celebration or another.''

Phillipa Raynes took a moment to beam in delight at the insinuation of an imminently successful marriage, as well as to bask in the appreciative glances of guests shrewd enough to understand exactly what Lady Raynes was suggesting. But then, her features slipped back into their general expression of having sniffed something foul without any idea of where the offensive odor might be coming from, and she protested, ''But we know nothing about her.''

''Nonsense,'' Lady Raynes was not about to allow her judgement to go contradicted in her own home, even by her own daughter. ''Miss Talbot comes to us with splendid references. After all, the Duchess of Hayley is one of my dearest friends, and she entrusted this girl with delivering her missive to us. Surely, there can be no higher recommendation.''

''Splendid idea, my lady.'' As far as Lord Raynes was concerned, the sooner they settled this silly business, the better. He had only just remembered a particularly tricky moment of negotiation between him and the dealer who'd sold him his precious gem, and he felt desperate to relay the tale before it once again slipped his mind. ''She can stay in one of the empty maid's rooms, can she not? Someone please show her the way, and, for God's sake, bring in the girl's clothes before she catches her death.''

"Oh, thank you. Thank you, Lord Raynes." For a moment, all the assembled guests expected the young lady to fall at his feet. Lord Raynes even drew both his legs in closer to his body, afraid of becoming splattered with muddy water.

Somehow, Lark fought the urge to fall prostrate, settling for dropping her umpteenth curtsey of the evening, and turning to silently follow the butler as he led her out of the salon and toward the back stairs.

Lady Raynes waited until both were well out of earshot before gaily telling her guests, "Don't let anyone ever suggest that Lord and Lady Raynes' parties lack drama."

"No," Damian said, his being the last pair of eyes to detach themselves from the path Miss Talbot had taken. "Nor intrigue."

Standing a mere stone's throw from the once royal city of Westminster, at almost the center of West End's most fashionable residential area, Mayfair, Lord and Lady Raynes' palatial town house boasted a kitchen in the basement, with windows looking out towards the fenced-in courtyard, a dining room and a salon on the ground floor, with a drawing room, billiard room, and library on the first, the master bedroom on the second, Miss Phillipa's suite of rooms on the third, and servants quarters above that. Each floor had its own series of stairs, plus a separate set in the back for the help.

With candle in hand, Lord and Lady Raynes' butler lectured Lark on the household's entire staff, consisting of himself, a housekeeper, four footmen, two coachmen, a groom, five housemaids, a handful—he couldn't quite recall the exact number, that was the housekeeper's job—kitchen-maids, and a constantly fluctuating figure of scullery-girls.

"I suspect Lord Raynes meant for you to take the former governess' room at the end of the hall, as Miss Phillipa is no longer in need of her services."

"Yes, sir. Thank you, sir."

The girl dragged her one miniature trunk of possessions behind her. Every time it banged against a stair, the butler winced, as if personally offended by the ungodly din.

"You will take your breakfast and dinner in the kitchen with the other servants. Lady Raynes will let you know when you shall be allowed a day off."

"Yes, sir. (Bang). Thank you, sir. (Bang)."

"Oh, do let me help you with that."

"Thank you, sir."

Lark accepted the candle he thrust at her in exchange for her trunk which he picked up onto his shoulders and carried the remainder of the distance to her room.

"There is coal by the fireplace. I trust that you are capable of keeping yourself warm without overturning the scuttle and creating a racket to wake the entire household."

"Yes, sir."

The door slammed tightly shut behind him.

She peeled off her wet clothes, grimacing at the cold, slimy way they clung to her arms and back, rubbing her hands together and blowing on them for warmth. Her flesh prickled with cold, the fingers slightly numb at the very tips.

After starting a fire on the grate, Lark crawled underneath the blankets which smelled vaguely damp. She pulled out her only drawing-pad from the bottom of the trunk, quickly sketching all she remembered of the salon and the back stairs.

She studied it closely, holding the faithful re-creation at arm's length, and then up close, turning it this way and that, and even upside down, until she felt confident that she'd memorized each and every detail.

Then, on a whim, Lark let her pen move in random geometric patterns, until, from beneath the squibbles, emerged a copy of Lady Raynes' beautiful ring, the diamond shimmering and sparkling in black and white, almost as much as it had under the salon chandelier's multiple lights.

Satisfied with her results, Lark braved the cold of climbing out from beneath her blankets and hurried barefoot across a floor colder than a frozen winter pond, to stand in front of the fireplace. She tossed her creations, one by one, into the flames, and forced herself to stand, shivering, until she'd made certain every scrap had burned into nothingness.

Only then did Lark allow herself the luxury of scampering back into bed and falling asleep.

She awoke to the sensation of being shaken, but there was no arm on her shoulder. The wind smacked an open window pane against the wall, making Lark jump and wonder how she hadn't noticed the open window before she fell asleep.

Outside, lighting cracked like a golden tree branch slapping the black sky, illuminating the clearly masculine figure sitting at the foot of Lark's bed, hands in his lap, fingers linked, waiting. The light outside painted his honey colored hair a rich molasses, and made his eyes glow in the darkness of her room.

"Please, Miss Talbot," said Damian Moxley. "There's no need to get up."

She inhaled sharply, pulling the blankets tighter around herself, and rolling over on her knees, ready to lunge like a cornered cat if necessary.

"I'd be careful, Miss Talbot. You've done so much gasping tonight, I wonder how you escaped asphyxiating."

"What do you want?" In back of her mind, Lark was already recalling the details of the Raynes house, guessing how loud a scream of hers might carry.

"To say hello." His voice remained steady, neutral, as if discussing a subject of no particular interest. "The party grew rather dull after you departed. You do know how to make an entrance, Miss Talbot."

"I know a lot of things, Mr. . . . ."

"Moxley. Damian Moxley."

"I shan't ask you again. What do you want?"

"To warn you, Miss Talbot."

"Warn me? Whatever about?"

"The Raynes diamond is mine. I have spent too much time and much too much effort maneuvering my proximity to the piece, to allow some nothing wench from Bath"—Lark could almost see his accent dropping social class by social class—"who's flaunting a ruse transparent enough to fool only the very dense or the very rich, to swoop in like a bloody vulture and take it from me. I intend for this to be your only warning, Miss Talbot. Leave my territory now, or pay the consequences."

2

"**Y**our territory? Your territory, is it? When exactly did the Prince Regent sign London over to you, pray tell?"

Now that she knew exactly what this late-night visit was all about, Lark felt no qualms about crawling out from beneath the blanket, and marching on her knees to confront Mr. Moxley until they were standing nearly face to face.

"I was working London whilst you were still in the schoolroom."

"Couldn't have been very long then, since the closest I ever came to books was having a bloke throw one at me out his window." Lark cocked her head to the side. "How did you wander up here, anyway? I hardly believe Lord Raynes lets his precious daughter's suitor have free rein wandering about the upstairs rooms."

Damian pointed to the open window. "I've climbed a roof or two in my day."

Lark couldn't stop the sympathy from creeping into her voice. "Chimney work, was it?"

She'd known enough unlucky sweeper's boys in her youth to fully imagine the horrors of that dubious profession. Sometimes, she still heard their screams in her sleep, begging, pleading, to be spared. And, no matter how bad things ever got with her, Lark always reassured herself with the knowledge that no back-breaking job could be as bad as being shoved into a still smoking chimney by a toothless sweep determined to get his money's worth.

"I was a different person, then." Damian pushed his hair off his forehead, as though the gesture might erase the memories that went with it.

Stripped of the civilized facade he'd been hiding behind while playing lap dog for Miss Phillipa, Damian Moxley appeared to grow bigger, straining against the tightness of his finely tailored clothes, as if desperate to break out and escape. Damian's damp blond hair rose in molehill spikes all about his scalp, giving him the look of a mischievous devil in training.

Lark sat back on her heels, crossed her hands and proceeded to study the man at arm's length, in much the same manner as she had her sketches a few hours earlier.

To all intents and purposes, he certainly resembled a well born young lord. His nails were finely manicured, the fingers long and limber, the palms soft and thoroughly devoid of any scars or blisters that might otherwise have suggested a working class past. Why, even his teeth were in fine order, gleaming white as they did in compliment to his bewitching eyes that languidly changed color from brown to green to near-yellow and back again.

"Are you daft, Miss Talbot?" Damian snapped his fingers in front of her face, making her briefly jump with surprise, before she regained her senses and slapped his hand away. "Did you not hear what I said? You are to leave this house tomorrow morning, and never so much as consider looking back."

Lark giggled. She couldn't help it. Men giving orders always did amuse her so. Especially when she considered how they expected those orders to be obeyed without question, as if the word had come down from God, rather than a mere mortal.

It reminded her of the boys she'd known at the flash house. Skinny, barefoot runts dressed in tatters who, nevertheless, somehow considered themselves worthy, obligated even, to issue orders to the women around them as if standing in for Napoleon at the Battle of Waterloo.

"Am I amusing you, Miss Talbot?" Damian grabbed her wrist, twisting hard enough to hurt, and pulling her towards him.

Lark refused to so much as wince, keeping the cheeky smile plastered to her face through sheer force of will, and then opening her mouth and letting out a blood-curdling scream loud enough to wake the dead—or, at the very least, Lord and Lady Raynes and their delightful daughter, Phillipa.

Within seconds, Damian had his hand clamped over her mouth and was slamming Lark back on the bed before the scream had a chance to fully clear her throat. He pinned her down, his elbows incapacitating her flailing arms, and straddling her with both his knees, sitting down on her stomach, so that Lark could only offer a few, futile kicks for defense.

His weight crushed down on her, squeezing the air out of Lark's lungs. She tried gasping for more, but Damian's hand rested so heavily across her mouth and nose, that Lark only managed to suck in her cheeks before coming to the horrible realization that he was attempting to choke her.

This wasn't like the boys she'd wrestled with in her youth, who, even at ages fifteen and sixteen got so little to eat that they barely outweighed her by half a stone.

And this wasn't like the country squires with whom she'd tangled in the past. There, no matter how angry a man got, he always remembered that he was a gentleman and she was a lady and that brought with it certain rules of conduct.

Damian Moxley obviously suffered from no such complexes.

He pressed his lips to her ear and whispered, "I will remove my hand from your face on the condition that you promise not to scream. If you do scream, I will snap your neck in a matter of seconds, and be out of this room before anyone even lights a candle and starts up the stairs. Tomorrow morning, you will be the topic of all the ladies' social calls in London. Everyone will agree what a ghastly thing it is that a young girl should be murdered in her bed. And then they will promptly forget all about you. Now, do you understand my terms? Nod your head if you understand.''

Feeling her head begin to spin and watching the bright colors burst in front of her eyes, Lark felt she had no choice but to nod.

Damian removed his hand.

She gulped gratefully, coughing so hard to clear her sandpaper-stuffed throat that her spasms shook Lark into a sitting position near eye level with Damian. He'd freed her face and arms, but remained perched where he was, across Lark's stomach, staring down at her with a combination of amusement and disgust.

She demanded, ''Would you bloody well get off of me.''

''Do you promise to behave?''

''Have you left me any choice?''

Damian smiled and languidly rolled over on his side, winking at Lark as he slowly removed his leg from her abdomen. ''I've never received any complaints before.''

''The unconscious rarely fuss.''

''Obviously you and I travel in very different social circles, Miss Talbot. Most of the young ladies of my acquaintance find that remaining conscious is a positive development.''

''Including Miss Phillipa?''

''Please. I said young ladies, not icicles.''

His humor struck her as particularly out of place considering their dangerous circumstances.

Furthermore, Lark prided herself on being a very sharp and speedy judge of character. She'd learned early on to relegate all people into easily defined compartments, and she hated it when a particular individual chose to straddle more than one category. If Damian Moxley wanted to seem menacing, then he should bloody well act consistently menacing, and refrain from muddying the waters with ill-timed bursts of humor.

Lark baited him, "You can't say anything detrimental about me to Lady Raynes, Mr. Moxley, you haven't an ounce of evidence."

"Oh, how I do enjoy being underestimated. What do you think, that I went from cleaning chimneys to being Designated Pet of the ton by backing down when the journey grew difficult?"

If truth be told, Lark was sincerely interested in learning precisely what journey it was that Damian Moxley had taken to achieve his present, lofty position. And she was even more interested in learning how she might duplicate such a feat.

Under different circumstances, she would have loved picking Damian's brain for a spot of financial advice. But instead, she merely announced, "You don't scare me. And if you expect that I should go running into the night simply because a flash-house boy in fine clothing tossed about a few threats, then it is you who underestimate me, Mr. Moxley."

"You are making a very big mistake."

"I enjoy taking risks. It puts the color in my cheeks, wouldn't you say?"

"That diamond is mine."

"We'll see about that, won't we? Now, please, run along, and close the window behind you. It's growing rather chilly in here."

Lark waited until she had seen Damian Moxley scurry down the side of the house and disappear into the night, before she allowed herself to experience sheer terror. He might have killed her right then. What kind of a fool was she, going up against a man willing to murder to get what he wanted?

There was no doubt Damian possessed more experience

in such matters of thievery than she did. Lark had never previously angled after a prize so precious. And certainly, her life had never been in such clear danger before.

Maybe it would be best to cut her losses and run. How hard, after all, would it be for Damian to do some research and turn up the information that while Lark had in fact served as secretary to the Duchess of Hayley, the letter directing Lark to the Stuarts was forged and that the duchess departed for India missing a trinket or two from her massive jewelry collection?

However, Lark refused to believe Damian Moxley had nothing to hide. Perhaps, instead of worrying about him finding her out, she should instead be focusing her energies on locating secrets to keep him in check. Or, better yet, get him completely out of the picture. Surely, Damian did not want his past revealed to the Rayneses anymore than Lark did.

And if there was one thing she had learned in her many years of criminal activity, it was that blackmail kept a mouth shut much better than any kind of pledged goodwill.

When Lady Raynes initially suggested that she might be in dire need of a secretary, Lark had no inkling of how prophetic her ladyship's words would prove.

She had barely reported for duty the next morning, when Lady Raynes presented Lark with a stack of fine stationery, a full inkwell, and a pair of pens. They, or rather Lark, would be writing out invitations for the Raynes' upcoming ball. Lark wondered if its purpose was so that the diamond might be introduced to the rest of London society.

Whilst Lark labored over the calligraphy, combating boredom by thinking of each letter as an independent work of art, Lady Raynes carried on a correspondence with her many friends and acquaintances residing in the country.

She wrote in a slow, graceful hand, accented by numerous flourishes. She needed to stop frequently to rest her fingers.

Lark said, "It must be ever so trying, attempting to write with such a weight upon your hand."

Lady Raynes glanced down at the ring, turning it so that the stone might better reflect the light. "In this life, my dear, one is called upon to make numerous sacrifices."

Lark bit her tongue and refrained from uttering the nearly half-dozen sarcastic rejoinders that dashed through her mind at that instant. Instead, she assumed her most innocent expression and asked, eyes open wide for effect, "Do you never remove your ring, Lady Raynes?"

"Goodness, no. I could never take such a risk. I am afraid I would spend every moment I had it out of my sight worried about thieves. I would never get a wink of sleep at night."

"You wear the ring to bed?" Lark wasn't quite quick enough to hide the disappointment in her tone. She hoped the slip had been misinterpreted as incredulity.

"It is the only way to feel certain it will remain in my possession. I do not mean to unduly frighten you, but I am afraid this city is full of unscrupulous sorts just laying in wait for a chance to get their hands on my precious gem."

The last thing Lark needed after a long day spent hunched over a writing desk was to hear a knock on her door, followed by a summons. If she had her way, the bulk of the evening would be spent soaking her aching right hand in a bowl of hot water until the joints in her fingers stopped cracking with every gesture. Both of Lark's shoulders throbbed, sending pinched lightning bolts down her spine.

What she wanted more than anything was a good night's sleep. What she got was the urgent message that Lord and Lady Raynes, along with Miss Phillipa and Mr.

Damian Moxley, were demanding her presence in the parlor that very instant.

Heart pounding, Lark all but flew down the back stairs, wondering what sort of horrid things Damian had told the Rayneses in her absence. She was already conjuring up excuses and explanations for her past exploits, when the parlor door opened and she was staring the Rayneses full in the face.

They did not look angry. Phillipa, for one, was positively glowing. But that, truly, could have meant anything.

Lark tried to read Damian's features, but, as with the first time they'd met, he'd somehow managed to blend into the background, conceding center-stage to his hosts. When Lark attempted to meet his gaze, he stubbornly looked away, linking arms with and focusing instead on the peculiarly euphoric Miss Phillipa.

"Wonderful news," she gushed to Lark. "Damian has come up with a solution to all of our problems. He's just dropped by to tell us that a business associate's wife is in desperate, immediate need of a personal secretary. Naturally, he thought of you first."

Lark just bet that he did.

Slowly, she said, "I wasn't aware that we had any problems. Was my work today below satisfactory, Lady Raynes?"

"What, dear? Why, certainly not."

"Then I am afraid I do not understand. Why am I being dismissed from your employ?"

"Come now, Miss Talbot." Phillipa stepped forward, still holding onto Damian's arm. "Surely, you understood that my mother's offering you food and lodging in exchange for services rendered was merely an act of charity. We could not have, in good conscience, tossed you out onto the street. But now that Damian has found a true employer willing to take you in—why, what could be better for all of us?"

For the first time since Lark had come in, Damian spoke up, his tone striking the perfect balance between gentlemanly courtesy and bored indifference. "My carriage is waiting outside, Miss Talbot. If you hurry and collect your things, I'll see to it that you're settled comfortably at your new residence by dinner time."

3

Lark's eyes met Damian's. "Why, Mr. Moxley, what a truly, truly generous gentleman you are. I can't fathom how I shall pay you back. For everything."

"I assure you, Miss Talbot, that no thanks need ever prove necessary. The delighted expression on your face is repayment enough for my efforts."

They both beamed at each other, until Lark imagined the glow from their insincerity could be visible through the windows. There might even be enough to illuminate all of London, throwing the gas lamp-lighters out of work. At the very least, people passing by on the street were probably wondering what those peculiar beams spilling from the Raynes' home were.

"Well," Phillipa said, "now that all is settled, perhaps Miss Talbot had best run along upstairs and fetch her things."

Lark nodded humbly, all the while imagining Phillipa's surprise if she ever learned just how far from settled the current situation truly was.

Lark felt certain that Damian thought he'd won this battle. He probably believed himself victor of the entire war. After all, with Lark out of the house, and him so firmly entrenched in it, his odds for being the first to reach Lady Raynes' diamond appeared unbeatable. But surrender had always been a rather awkward word in Lark's vocabulary. Her tongue refused to pronounce it, and her limbs never quite managed to do it. It was a stance borne of foolish courage. And desperation. If Lark lost her access to the Raynes' diamond, it might be months before she set up another victim. And she had no place else to go in the meantime. The idea of spending half a year doing tedious secretarial work, without even the simultaneous adventure of plotting a theft, made Lark feel ill. She'd first return to scrounging for coal and copper nails among the shallow banks of the Thames along with the other mudlarks, before getting trapped in a life of middle-class monotony.

Lark turned to Lady Raynes and dropped yet another curtsey on the assumption that an overdone show of humility never hurt anything. Lark said, "My gratitude for your kindness knows no end, my lady. My one regret is of abandoning you whilst there still remains so much work yet to be done."

Lady Raynes' eyebrows narrowed and she brought one hand to her face. Resting her chin atop her middle finger and rubbing her cheek with the index, she recalled the mountains of invitations Lark had only started addressing that morning.

Lark offered, "Mayhap I had best leave a list of written instruction for your new girl regarding how you prefer your affairs handled, Lady Raynes. After all, there is no need to waste your valuable time repeating instructions to each new employee."

Predictably, Damian proved the first person to grasp what Lark was attempting to do, and he rushed to intercept her efforts. "Lady Raynes managed matters just fine before your arrival, Miss Talbot. I feel confident that she will prove able to carry on equally as effectively after you leave."

"Oh, I do not doubt that for an instant, Mr. Moxley." Lark smiled reassuringly at Lady Raynes. "But still, I would feel ever so much less guilty about abandoning you in such a manner, if her Ladyship might allow me a few moments prior to departure to sort the invitations into those that go out immediately, and those that we might discreetly hold until the positive and negative responses are tallied. Oh, yes, and with your permission, I've noticed that there is a certain style of penmanship preferred. Your own design, is it, Lady Raynes? Very elegant. Permit me to leave an alphabet of examples for your new girl, so that she might begin practicing to imitate it as soon as possible.''

"Come now, Miss Talbot." Even without an explanation from Damian, Phillipa was beginning to grasp the situation. "Do you really believe such fuss is necessary? After all, you managed to absorb all of my mother's requirements in less than a day.''

"And, believe me, Phillipa, she is the first to do so." Instead of feeling reassured by her daughter's protestations, Lady Raynes appeared to grow more agitated by the second. "My darling, you simply have no concept of how difficult it is to locate a girl capable of following all my instructions. Truly, it was that exact hardship that prompted me to forgo hiring a secretary altogether these last few months. I simply grew weary of constantly looking over their shoulders and then still needing to redo all work at the end of the day. Why, Miss Talbot was a godsend. I don't know how I shall ever manage without her now.''

"Well, that settles it then." Lord Raynes, who previously hadn't an opinion one way or the other on Miss Talbot's future employment, now refused to deprive his wife of such an obviously necessary accessory. "The girl stays. Moxley, tell your friend we're sorry, but Miss Talbot has proven herself most indispensable to this household, and we simply can not let her go at this juncture. Better luck next time and all that.''

"Yes." Lark caught Damian's eye, hoping he could read her triumphant thoughts. "Better luck next time, Mr. Moxley.''

To his credit, Damian accepted Lord Raynes' procla-
mation without further protest. Although naturally, Lark
didn't fool herself into thinking it was due to any gentlemanly instincts on Damian's part. He was simply too good
a game player to press on with a losing hand. Now all
Lark had to do was wait and wonder what he might show
up bearing next.

Only Lark had no intention of sitting by passively while
he plotted to destroy her. She'd picked up a trick or two
in her day.

After all, Mr. Damian Moxley wasn't the only Raynes'
visitor who'd travelled the road from sewer rat to respectability in the space of some twenty odd years.

Lark Talbot's earliest memories were of standing, barefoot and thigh-deep, in the Thames River at low-tide. She
couldn't recall how she'd gotten there or who might have
brought her. All Lark remembered was plunging her arms
as deep as she could into the mud, and feeling around for
stray bits of rope or bone. She arched her back and stuck
her chin up in the air, trying to avoid swallowing dirt. It
hurt to breathe in that position, but she didn't dare move
around much. The river floor was covered with glass and
nails. One wrong step, and she could slice the inside of
her foot in half.

On a good day, the scavenging for loose odds and ends
might bring in as much as a threepence from the rag-and-
bone man, so Lark arrived early and stayed until sundown.
Afterwards, she followed the other mudlarks to a nearby
steam factory, where they stood in the waste stream of
hot water, jumping up and down, struggling to return sensation to their frozen legs.

Even the orange girls and the girls who sold bootlaces
on the street looked down at the mudlarks. They teased
them about being dirty and started shouting, "Stop,
thief," if one so much as stood too close to their precious
wares.

Crossing sweepers hated to see mudlarks on their corners. They claimed it made their job of brushing away mud and dust from the street so that the ladies and gentlemen might not get their feet dirty, even harder, what with the grimy mudlarks trailing their filth wherever they went.

Lark got so used to being recognized and addressed by her livelihood, that, by the time she grew big enough to dream of escaping her life and finding another, she could no longer recall ever having responded to any different, proper name.

It was the piemen who first offered Lark a chance out of the mud. A majority of them subscribed to the practice of letting customers flip coins for their supper. If the pieman guessed heads or tails right, he took the penny and the buyer went hungry. If he guessed wrong, the customer got his pie for free.

As a rule, Lark tried to stay away from such gambles. With a salary of maybe threepence a day, she couldn't afford to risk one third her income on chance. But that was before Lark learned the tricks of the trade.

She taught herself a simple slight of hand by diligently practicing in front of a splintered mirror someone had thrown out with the trash. All she needed were two pennies. One face up, and one face down. She couldn't lose.

Within a few weeks, Lark was making the rounds of every pieman in London. She won more apple, currant, gooseberry, beef, and mutton pies than one ten year old girl could possibly eat in a day, and promptly resold the leftovers. Lark was operating on pure profit. By the end of the year, she'd earned enough to invest in clean clothes, a comb for her hair, and a hot bath. Looking as respectable as a former mudlark could ever hope to get, she took a job as a scullerymaid for a fine family in Mayfair.

From sunup to sundown, she was relegated to the kitchen, scrubbing the unending stream of pots, pans, and dishes that returned from the dining room following every breakfast, nuncheon, tea, dinner, supper, and evening tea service.

In retrospect, Lark often thought that the only difference between her work as a mudlark and as a scullerymaid was that, in one, she'd stood drenched to the thighs in freezing mud, while in the other she stood drenched to the elbows in scalding water. While once her legs turned blue from the cold, now her arms grew crimson from the heat. The skin about her nails peeled and ripped, turning into bloody scabs that stung from the cleaning soda.

And, most infuriating of all, the upper servants, the housemaids and the kitchenmaids, were even more cruel in their treatment of her than Lark had ever experienced while living on the street. They laughed at her attempts to balance a half-dozen saucepans stacked one on top the other, and tried to trip Lark as she carried them. She suspected that they deliberately set out more plates than could possibly be necessary, for a meal for the pleasure of seeing Lark buried in work, still scrubbing at her post long after midnight.

Respectability, Lark learned quickly enough, was a fine concept. But it only worked if you had the money to sit at the top of the ladder, looking down at everybody else.

So she felt no qualms about stealing. Her victims possessed a lot, she possessed a little, and it was all in the name of fairness, after all. Did not the ministers at the church she was forced to attend every Sunday preach about fairness and charity and sharing? As far as Lark was concerned, she was doing God's work. And that was exactly the sentiment she repeated to herself on those nights when her conscience made sleep difficult.

In the ten years since she'd begun plying her dubious trade, Lark did not doubt that she had made some enemies who would be happy to speak badly of her . . . if only they knew whom to address their complaints to. So far, she had managed to move around often enough to avoid being caught.

She expected it to be the same with Damian Moxley. No one could rise from squirming chimney boy to the owner of London's largest factory without taking an unlawful detour or two.

And Lark was determined to not only dig up Damian's past, but to come serving it, steaming hot, right to the Raynes' doorstep.

Lark's second day in Lady Raynes' employ might have proven as numbingly tedious as her first, were it not for her ongoing attempts to learn more about Damian.

While helping Lady Raynes sort through the calling cards that arrived during that morning's visit hours, Lark inquired, with wide-eyed, breathless romanticism, how Miss Phillipa and Mr. Moxley first became acquainted.

Lady Raynes' brow furrowed into the consternation common to all mothers raising particularly difficult children, and she confessed, "Phillipa and I visited Mr. Moxley's factory one afternoon in search of a chandelier for the ballroom. Lady Benson had purchased a spectacular specimen the previous month and she simply could not stop raving about their excellent crystal workmanship. Why, she hired them on the spot to design an original series of wine glasses for her granddaughter's debut. Well, naturally, we had to take a look for ourselves. As soon as Mr. Moxley heard that Phillipa and I were on the premises he insisted on coming down from his office to help with our selection."

"And that was it then," Lark observed, more to herself than to Lady Raynes. "That was the beginning."

"Unfortunately. I saw the way that young man looked at my Phillipa. He simply could not take his eyes off her. I told my husband he would come calling soon, and surely enough, the very next evening, there was Mr. Moxley. Oh, his lordship was terribly cross. Phillipa is his only child, naturally, he wants the very best for her. Why, he even sent away the Earl of Leavitt's boy because he was a younger son, and his lordship has no use for gentlemen without a hope of ever inheriting."

"Is Mr. Moxley a peer then?" For a moment, Lark wondered if she might have gotten everything all muddled. What if Damian Moxley were actually an aristocrat?

"Oh, no. And believe me, my dear, that deficit on his part caused such grief about this household. Why, there were nights I could barely sleep at all."

"I can only imagine."

Lady Raynes sighed. "But Phillipa—I do not know if you have noticed—can be quite headstrong. And once she set her sights on Mr. Moxley—he is a handsome devil, no argument. Why, if I were twenty years younger—well, there was no talking her out of it. His Lordship, of course, wanted that basket scrambler tossed out on his ear the first day. Imagine Damian Moxley's cheek, coming to court the daughter of Lord Raynes, no less! But it was I who talked Archie out of making a scene. I know my child. If we had fussed over the impropriety of it all, Phillipa would have only clung to her Mr. Moxley that much tighter. She does enjoy acting devilish. But I have faith. My Phillipa is not foolish enough to make any sort of promise to a man of Mr. Moxley's ilk. It's a game she's playing, mark my words. She's having a bit of fun with us. Phillipa understands as well as anyone that Damian could never be accepted among civilized peoples. Even if his affluence does eventually lead to a knighthood for services to the Crown."

Lark tried to imagine Damian Moxley being knighted. She hoped the Prince Reagent planned to place all his valuables under lock and key for the occasion.

She chose her next words very carefully, struggling to project innocent curiosity and sincere befuddlement, while, at the same time, digging determinedly toward a useful response. "How is it then that a gentleman outside of the peerage has managed to do so well for himself financially?"

The question left Lady Raynes genuinely puzzled. She stopped what she was doing, dropping the remaining calling cards back in the bowl, arms on her hips, and peered directly at Lark. The diamond stared at Lark, too, taunting her into continuing the inquiry, while common sense suggested she step back for a bit. There was no use in appearing unduly interested in Damian Moxley. Phillipa was already suspicious enough. The last thing Lark wanted to do was provoke her mother.

For a beat she and Lady Raynes stood at stalemate, two pairs of eyes staring at each other, wondering what to say next.

Finally, Lady Raynes waved Lark's question away with a toss of her bejeweled hand. The frown that briefly crossed her features was instantly replaced with a smile, and she shook her head at Lark. "It is my opinion that such financial matters are best left to the men. Figures and funds and counsels, such a dull business. Why, I simply die of boredom whenever I hear men discussing them."

She'd lost her chance, Lark could clearly see that. Any attempt to return the conversation toward Damian Moxley and his questionable fortune now would be obvious prying. Lark couldn't take the risk no matter how badly she may have wanted to.

She sighed. This was the most difficult part of any job. The slow, painstaking gathering of information. She hated it with a passion. In the end, Lark found she spent more time sitting about and waiting, than actually acting. Nervous energy built up inside of her like steam in a kettle. It made her want to do something drastic, simply to make the buzzing in her head lessen. She felt wound up so tightly, it took every ounce of self-control that Lark possessed to keep from jumping at each loud noise, or flying to the ceiling if someone so much as brushed up against her. She'd heard of thieves being described as possessing itchy fingers. Well, hers didn't just itch, they hummed.

It had always been like this, and Lark had learned to cover up her nerves in the same way that she hid all of her other emotions. Yet just because she did not seem anxious on the outside, did not mean the waiting wasn't driving her mad.

It had taken Lark two months to set up the circumstances of her arrival at the Raynes' household, and now who knew how long it might take before she was in a position to abscond with the ring.

The only problem was, she'd never raced against an opponent before. It tripled her risk of capture, and lowered the odds of success. Lark couldn't work this way. It was too distracting.

Damian was too distracting.

She needed to be rid of him, and quickly, before the tables turned and she found herself out on the street for good.

4

Lark supposed that if she were being reasonable, she would concede that the best person to pump for information about Damian Moxley, was, in fact, Damian Moxley.

He was in possession of every bit of information she would ever need. The trick, of course, was to pry it out of him.

She had to confront him. There was no getting around the fact. Confront him on grounds a bit more neutral than her darkened bedroom, with Damian's hand clamped across her mouth. Unfortunately, Lark could conceive of no site at which Damian still did not hold an advantage. Certainly not at the Raynes' home, where, at any moment, he might expose her charade. And never on the street. It wouldn't be proper.

Finally, Lark decided on the factory. There, at least, they would be chaperoned, albeit superficially, by the other employees. And she felt certain that Damian would not physically harm her there. It would be too awkward to explain.

So the factory it would have to be. Except for one minor problem. Lark was afraid to see Damian again.

Well, not afraid exactly. Afraid was what she had felt when she believed him capable of choking her. This sensation was different. She felt apprehensive. Something about Damian Moxley made her nervous. She remembered the way he'd looked at her that first evening, as if he knew exactly what she were thinking and feeling. And he were amused by it all.

He did possess a most annoying habit of acting as if he found everything funny, although he never, as far as Lark could tell, actually laughed. It unnerved her. Rather like the way his unexpected swerve from menacing to humorous these two nights past had. It threw Lark off balance. How in the world was one supposed to control a person who insisted on being so bloody unpredictable?

That was the problem with Damian. Most other people, Lark could grasp in an instant. She knew within minutes of saying her first hello, who they were, what they wanted, and how they could best be manipulated. But not Damian. She couldn't understand him at all. Why should a man already so well off that the peerage considered him valid son-in-law material wish to risk losing so much in exchange for so little?

In Lark's case, selling the Raynes diamond would give her enough money to escape England for a comfortable life in India or America. Someplace where no one knew her and, more importantly, no one could find her. But even the highest bidder on the market could never offer Damian more for the diamond than his factory was worth. So why then was he taking these hideous risks? Was the man mad? Lark certainly hoped not. It was ever so difficult to blackmail the insane.

And yet she had to try.

She needed to gather enough incriminating information on Damian to, at the very least, force him to relinquish those blasted proprietary claims he still held on *her* diamond.

There was no way around it. Lark needed to seek out Damian Moxley. The only problem was, how to do so without arousing any unnecessary suspicions. Especially on the Rayneses' part.

* * *

"Oh, I am so terribly sorry. Do forgive me." Lark gasped and dove under the table. On her knees, she hurriedly tried to brush the broken lamp shards into her hands, cutting both palms in the process. "I don't know how I could have been so clumsy. Your beautiful crystal lamp, ruined."

The tears springing to Lark's eyes, as well as the blood on her skin, were genuine. With her thumb, she'd deliberately driven a piece of cracked glass into her palm.

"You clumsy girl." Lady Raynes' exasperated rebuke seemed to address itself not only to Lark, but to every other accident-prone servant ever hired. Why, oh why, was good help so hard to find?

"You must let me replace it for you, Lady Raynes."

"Of that, you may feel certain, Miss Talbot. I will see to it that my husband deducts the amount from your salary each week—"

"That won't be necessary. I shall go right now to Mr. Damian Moxley's factory and purchase you another lamp identical to the one I broke. I have some money saved. I won't be long, I promise. Oh, do forgive me, Lady Raynes."

And Lark was out the door, heading for Damian's, before the lady of the house had so much as a chance to reply.

The ground floor of Damian Moxley's factory served as his shop as well. Through the front window, Lark spied a display of cut glass, inkwells, plates, mirrors, chandeliers, figurines and lamps. A sign advertised all items to be available for sale, with special custom orders also taken. A clerk met Lark at the door, inquiring how he might be of assistance.

Lark told him, adding that the lamp she wished to purchase was for the Raynes household and suggesting that Mr. Moxley might like to be included in the transaction.

The clerk disappeared behind a grey door in the back

of the shop. Before it closed, Lark caught a glimpse of long worktables surrounded by craftsmen, their shoulders hunched over incomplete sculptures. A fire blazed in the distance, while a row of men blew what looked to be soap bubbles through skinny black tubes.

Damian appeared a few moments later, the sleeves of his coat covered by a shiny dust Lark recognized as crystal.

"Why, Miss Talbot," he bowed deeply. "To what do I owe such an unexpected honor?"

His exuberance surprised Lark, as did his seemingly casual nature. But, then again, it really should not have. Surrounded by inventory, Damian Moxley was truly master of all he surveyed. And the knowledge, naturally, affected his demeanor. No longer the excruciatingly polite fancy man hoping to make an impression on his young lady's parents, Damian positively glowed with a robust self-confidence. For the first time since they had met, Lark noticed that his skin finally seemed to fit him. He no longer resembled a swiftly growing boy poised to explode out of his shrunken Sunday-best suit at any moment. Lark wondered how Miss Phillipa could have seen her almost-intended in his natural surroundings, and possibly not prefer him to the pale, diluted imitation he turned into when out and about among the ton.

So affected was Lark to witness yet another side to Damian's perpetually metamorphosing personality, that she needed to take a beat before answering. "It is as I told your clerk. I broke Lady Raynes' table lamp. I need to purchase a replacement."

"Of course. Well, we have a fine selection to choose from." Damian walked to a shelf loaded with assorted glass bric-a-bracs, gesturing across the width. "What do you want?"

He managed to infuse the four simple words with so many levels of meaning, Lark wasn't sure which to answer first.

Yet, convinced that while they stood alone in the shop,

no one could overhear or come to disturb them, she plugged ahead with the true purpose of her visit. "A bit of illumination, sir."

"What you see here is all that I currently have in stock."

"Oh, I do doubt that very much. I wager a gentleman of your sort keeps quite a bit in the back, out of view, for shortages and emergencies and the like."

Again the amused smile. Only now, Lark thought she spied just a touch of professional admiration as well. He replied, "Indeed. But the luxury items are well hidden and only available for the most special of inquiries. They must be commissioned in advance. Besides, in order for the customer to feel fully satisfied with what he—or she— has received, one must first know exactly what it is they are looking for."

"Of that you need have no fear, sir. I arrived knowing."

Damian sighed deeply, taking a step back and contemplating Lark from a distance, the way an artist might survey his chosen subject. For a moment, there was something almost paternal in his gaze—a master craftsman gazing fondly at a particularly gifted protege. But the affection did not last long.

Unexpectedly, Damian clapped both his hands together. The noise made a few of the glassworks nearest to him bounce on their shelves. He spoke bruskly. "This has grown tedious. Some of us have jobs to do. So either spit out your piece or go home considering the entire fishing trip a failure."

Exasperated, for she was just starting to hope that clever word games might prove the route to forcing Damian into saying more than he meant to, Lark exclaimed, "I do not understand you. Here you've managed to acquire a business others would chop their right and left eyes out for, and yet you are willing to risk losing it. What in the world are you after?"

"More," Damian said simply. "I want more. If one

factory is good, then two is better, and three is divine. My business makes money. But not enough to expand at the rate I'm interested in.''

"So you supplement your income with a bit of thievery.''

Damian snorted. "Pay close attention, Miss Talbot, since this is not likely to come up again in ordinary conversation. What you engage in, lifting a bauble or two from some senile old lady's jewelry box, is thievery. What I do, is an art known as larceny.''

Lark haughtily tossed her head. "I'm sorry if I insulted you. Little did I know you took such pride in your profession.''

Damian smiled, but the expression died at the corners of his mouth without reaching the eyes. "You are such an innocent. Why don't you go back to the provinces. I am sure you earned quite a fine living there. Why, with a little luck, you might even marry, and spend the rest of your days pilfering your husband's pockets. You're not a bad looking sort. It could happen.''

She couldn't be certain. Was Damian complimenting her? His words implied as much, and yet his tone and manner suggested quite the opposite. Lark was accustomed to receiving her compliments with smiles, and usually from gentlemen whose intentions loomed much clearer than Damian's.

"Yes,'' Damian said.

"I beg your pardon?'' While she struggled to discern his meaning, Lark was disgusted to feel herself blushing nevertheless.

"Yes, I did offer you a compliment.''

"Oh.''

"Don't think too much of it. I was merely stating a fact.''

The red in her cheeks slid to anger. "Don't worry. My daily calendar hardly called for swooning at your feet.''

"I am *so* happy to hear of it.''

"I believe that is Miss Phillipa's job. You certainly

have her wrapped tightly around your smallest finger. I would wager she hardly suspects that you are nothing more than a basket scrambler.''

Damian crossed both arms against his chest. ''Are you, of all people, offering a judgement on my actions? That's showing a bit of cheek, isn't it? Am I supposed to believe that you've never traded on your feminine charms to hit the bulls-eye?''

''That was different.''

''Why?''

''Because. When I do it, it's fair. In case it has slipped by your notice, Mr. Moxley, it is a man's world out there, and feminine charm is the only weapon a lady has to even up the odds a bit. But it is not right for a gentleman to toy with a lady's affections. Not when he has so many other tools at his disposal. It isn't fair to steal away our only advantage. It isn't.''

Finally, Damian laughed. His chin dropped to his chest, and his shoulders shook. He covered his face with both hands, looking at Lark from above his fingers, still laughing.

''Just what is so funny?'' she demanded.

''Hypocrisy, Miss Talbot.'' Damian's eyes danced, magically spiraling through their brown and green spectrum, as he explained, ''I do find it terribly amusing. Especially among the so-called civilized classes. All those social niceties . . . Always give a lady the wall, always ride backward in a carriage with a lady, never smoke in the presence of a lady, always precede a lady going up the stairs . . . So many rules for superficial conduct, whilst underneath simmers cruel intrigue the likes of which even common criminals like you and I could take a lesson from. Well, maybe not I. But you certainly could learn a thing or two.''

Blue-deviled by his bamming, her first instinct was to turn and walk out, but she fought the urge to fly into the boughs. That was exactly what Damian wanted her to do. He wanted to get her angry, so that she might forget her goals. Well, Lark wasn't about to give him the satisfaction.

After all, she could gammon along with the best of them. She asked, "Have you given much thought to the possibility that you might end up losing everything? If Lord and Lady Raynes learn you are plotting to rob them, you'll not only lose the diamond, but Phillipa and the factory as well. When word of your true nature gets out, you won't have a customer left."

"I have no intention of getting caught."

"Still," Lark pressed, "once you flee London with the diamond, what will become of your factory?"

"Did I say anything about fleeing London? Please do not confuse your childish plot with my well thought-out plan. I have no intention of going anywhere."

"But surely, once the jewel disappears, you'll be a prime suspect in the theft. You won't be able to sell it in London."

"An amateur." Damian sighed and shook his head sadly. As if he'd for a moment expected more of her, but then had his original assumption of inferiority confirmed. "Please, Miss Talbot, take my advice. Set your sights on something a tad more within your reach. I would hate to see what becomes of that pretty little face of yours after a decade in Newgate prison."

The nervous energy that Lark fought so hard to keep under control bubbled at his words, pressing against her skin like a million pins in search of an exit. "And I suppose you think becoming the Rayneses' son-in-law will keep you above suspicion?"

"If that's what you believe, then I am willing to play along with such a theory."

"You'd actually marry Phillipa? Just to get the diamond?" Somehow, the realization lowered her opinion of Damian. Lark had thought many things of him in the past few days, but, at the very least, she'd clung to the hope that he might harbor some standards of decency, if not taste.

The merriment of a moment earlier drained from Damian's face. He lowered both arms, sliding them in the pockets of his trousers and leaning back on his heels, lips set in a dark line. "I would never allow myself to be forced into a loveless marriage. No matter what the circumstances."

Lark swallowed hard, unsure of how to respond. His intensity frightened her on a level much different than his ambiguity had. It reminded her of the way he'd looked while threatening to snap her neck. It made her wonder of the violence Damian might prove capable of if sufficiently provoked.

His outburst cost Lark her chance for any more prodding. Without another word, Damian opened the door and summoned his clerk, ordering the young man to take care of Lark's purchase.

Then, after sending his best wishes to the Raynes family, Damian disappeared back into the work area, leaving Lark to curse her lack of tact and lost opportunity.

On the ride back home, lamp carefully wrapped and stored under the carriage seat, Lark faced the hard fact that she would, in all likelihood, be needing to scrap her plans for blackmailing Damian Moxley. Without anything to go on, she hadn't the faintest idea where to start digging up his past. She could hardly embark on a house to house search, asking every aging chimney sweep whether he'd once made the acquaintance of a youth named Damian Moxley.

Well then, Lark folded her hands in her lap and squared both shoulders in what she liked to think of as her battle posture. She'd never been one to cry over spilled milk, and if her initial plan had proven itself impossible, well, that only meant it was time to move on to another, more practical plot.

If she couldn't blackmail Damian into keeping his distance, then she could certainly try to keep him as physically far away from the Raynes diamond as possible.

And the only way Lark could conceive of to do that, was to keep Damian away from Miss Phillipa.

Permanently.

When she arrived home, she handed Lady Raynes the replacement lamp accompanied by a stream of apologies and promises that it would never happen again. She kept her head bowed low, so that Lady Raynes could not help but see the tears Lark was struggling so valiantly to keep hidden.

Naturally, the lady of the house protested. "Such grief for a mere lamp? Come now, I have already forgotten the morning's mishap, and I feel it would be best for you to do the same."

Lark nodded miserably. "You have been so kind to me, Lady Raynes. So kind. That is why I stand so torn now. Surely, my first loyalty lies with you and your family. But what if I am mistaken? It is hardly my place to cast suspicion—"

"Suspicion?" Lady Raynes' hand flew to the lace at her neck. "What are you saying, Miss Talbot? Suspicion of whom?"

"Oh, I've said too much already." Lark turned away, her shoulders heaving with a series of most convincing sobs.

"In this house, my dear," Lady Raynes dropped her solicitous tone in favor of a firmer, mistress-addressing-the-help sort, "we finish what we start. I won't have any unanswered intrigue polluting my home with its foul stench. Tell me what it is that you suspect, so that we might get on with our work."

Lark took a deep breath, the anxiety in her voice now totally sincere. She knew that once she said the words, there would be no turning back. By putting this particular plan into motion, Lark was risking everything. Her heart sped up its beating and she smiled inwardly, enjoying the familiar sensation of molten energy surging through her veins, making Lark feel invincible. In this state, she understood exactly why it was that drunks returned nightly to their pub stools, why soldiers marched into battle even after being wounded, why squires continued hunting game when they could surely afford to engage others for the dirty work. It was the closest sensation Lark could imagine to flying. And, if she were truly honest with herself, she might even admit that it was this feeling, perhaps even more than the financial remunerations, that kept her tracking other people's belongings long after she'd accumulated an adequate-for-survival balance at her bank.

But Lark knew better than to let Lady Raynes spot even a fraction of what she was thinking. When Lark turned back to her mistress, it was with tear-stained cheeks and a trembling chin. In a small voice, Lark managed to choke out, "It's Mr. Moxley, my lady. I'm afraid I possess evidence suggesting that he's being unfaithful to Miss Phillipa."

5

Lady Raynes wrestled with a conundrum.

In theory, etiquette dictated righteous indignation, followed by a firm rebuke and a speedy dismissal of the young chit cheeky enough to bring her such an accusation. But there was a minor problem. Lady Raynes' lifelong love of gossip, combined with a genetic distrust of anyone not to the manner born, even a well-off cit like Damian Moxley, was racing a good seven or eight miles ahead of her otherwise impeccable sense of social propriety. Lady Raynes desperately wanted to hear everything Lark had to say.

She hid it, of course. It simply would not do to have the help privy to her thoughts and weaknesses.

So Lady Raynes feigned casualness as she instructed Lark, "I dearly hope you have come armed with evidence to support your thoroughly outlandish claim."

Lark wanted to leap in the air for joy. Her bomb had hit its intended target. All that was left now was to make certain no one snuffed out the fuse.

She coughed, pretending to clear her throat. In actuality, Lark was forcing a hoarse lump in, not out, of her voice. That added a lovely touch when it cracked in the middle of a confession.

"I was at Mr. Moxley's factory, my lady, searching to replace the lamp I so clumsily shattered this morning."

"Yes, yes, I'm quite aware of all that. Do get on with the remainder of the tale."

"Of course." Lark linked all ten of her fingers primly in front of her, and brought both hands up to her chin, almost as if in prayer. "There were a pair of gentlemen in the shop. Well, I truly can't say whether or not they were gentlemen. Employees of Mr. Moxley, that's what they were. Lower class sorts, I would presume. Not even clerks or the like. Although, it is hard to tell. All of Mr. Moxley's employees wear the same uniform. Blue smocks to protect their clothes from the dust. But it does make it rather hard to differentiate among them, so—"

"Come now, Miss Talbot. We are not living in a novel. It is not necessary for you to describe every stick of furniture in the room before you tell me what went on there."

She sensed Lady Raynes growing frustrated with the tension Lark was working so hard to build into her tale, and she decided to cut the rest of her scene setting short, lest she miscalculate and overplay her advantage.

Skipping straight to the end, Lark told Lady Raynes, "Once the gentlemen heard that it was a lamp for the Raynes' household that I was looking to purchase, I heard a great deal of whispering from them. Most of it quite ribald and not fit to repeat in decent company."

"Oh?" Lady Raynes sounded truly disappointed with that latest bit. But she was too much of a lady to let it show.

"The gist of it, your ladyship, concerned Mr. Moxley and your daughter. And a certain young lady who visits him every day after work, before he comes to call on Phillipa."

There. She had gotten it all out in more or less the fashion Lark had planned. The next step was Lady Raynes'. There was only so close to the water that Lark could lead this horse, after all. The final sip would be up to her.

Lady Raynes took a moment to digest the latest information. She cocked her head and looked at Lark from the side, debating how much credence to lend her words. Thoroughly at home under the harsh lights of a suspicious stare, Lark gazed back innocently.

When she had formulated this scene in her head on the way back from Damian's factory, Lark had composed her own dialogue, along with Lady Raynes' responses, and she was pleased to see how closely they'd both followed the script.

Now that things had reached their critical point, Lark had a few ideas on what Lady Raynes' next move might be, and she felt confident in her ability to adjust to any option.

Except for the one that Lady Raynes actually chose.

Grabbing Lark by the arm, she pulled her out of the room and down the hall, calling for Phillipa.

Lark cursed her stupid miscalculation.

She had felt certain that Lady Raynes would not want to upset her daughter by involving Phillipa in the rumor so early in the game. If Lark had her way, Phillipa would never even find out about the accusation. All she would have known was that Damian Moxley was no longer welcome in the house, and that would be that. In the most extreme case, Lark could have dealt with Phillipa eventually being told—but only after Lord and Lady Raynes were fully convinced of the truthfulness of Lark's words.

This way, Lark would be forced to convince the two women simultaneously. A much harder task, especially considering that both stood already predisposed to doubting her.

Phillipa looked up, her lips wrinkling in distaste, as soon as she spotted Lark. She'd been sitting in front of her mirror, diligently brushing back strands of hair so blond, Lark thought she detected a greenish tinge.

When they entered, Phillipa did not bother to turn, preferring instead to continue sitting with her back to them, and addressing their reflections in the mirror.

Although intensely focused on the hard row to hoe ahead, Lark allowed herself a brief moment to look sideways at the bedroom's decor, and come to the instantaneous conclusion that she had never seen so much useless bric-a-brac crowded onto shelves, outside of a Bond Street shop. If it was eye-catching and, preferably, gilt-edged and gold-plated, Phillipa owned it. She wondered briefly if some of the items had been gifts from Damian, then quickly rejected the idea. Even judging solely on the merchandise manufactured at his factory, Lark could comfortably say that Damian possessed much better taste. If he had given Phillipa any of these items, it would had to have been as a sly joke only he was privy to.

Lady Raynes filled her daughter in on the disturbing news about Damian, using as few words as possible. The entire time, she kept Lark in front of her, almost as a shield. It made Lark wonder whether Lady Raynes weren't a bit frightened of her daughter.

"You are a filthy liar, Miss Talbot." Finally, Phillipa deigned to grace them with her full attention. She spun around, half-rising out of her chair. "How dare you say such things about a fine man like Mr. Moxley?"

Phillipa's spirited defense surprised Lark. After her chat with Lady Raynes, where the older woman flatly stated her family's consensus on Damian's undesirability, she had expected Phillipa to show little concern over the potential loss of a man she had no true serious interest in, in the first place. If Phillipa was merely toying with Damian to throw a shock into the ton, then revelation of his infidelity ought to have been exactly the nudge she needed to end the game and move on to a more acceptable suitor.

Lark turned to Lady Raynes. "I was only repeating what I heard. You have been so kind to me. I would hate to see—"

"The only thing you would hate to see, Miss Talbot, is my marriage to Mr. Moxley. You think that I have not noticed the interest you have taken in him. Asking my mother questions about his past, using every opportunity to run off to his factory.''

On her internal scorecard, Lark chalked up an extra point for Miss Phillipa. The girl was much sharper than she seemed. Even if her conclusions were erroneous, at least she'd picked up the signs.

Which was more than Lark had done. She'd failed to understand that Phillipa may not have been interested in Damian for the long term, but she would be damned if she allowed him to make a fool of her in front of the ton, by throwing Phillipa over for another woman. It would be one thing for Phillipa to dismiss the man, and laugh with her friends about the social-climbing pretensions of the working-class. It would be quite another for a member of the working class to declare her unworthy.

Lady Raynes laughed. ''Don't be silly, darling. Miss Talbot and Mr. Moxley? What an absurd idea. Whatever even made you think of such a thing?''

''What other reason would she have for making up this vicious lie, Mama?''

''It isn't a lie.'' Lark stood firm, hoping the impression she'd made on Lady Raynes would be enough to sway her daughter.

''I should like to see some proof then.'' Phillipa planted both hands on her hips. Lark supposed it was the closest a lady of her station could come to making fists.

''Yes.'' Lady Raynes leapt upon the solution as if solving a squabble between two children. ''Did you not say, Miss Talbot, that this woman the gentlemen at the factory spoke of, visits Mr. Moxley every day after work?''

''Yes.'' Lark couldn't be sure where Lady Raynes' trail of thought was leading, and the prospect made her very nervous.

''Splendid. We shall simply travel to the factory at the appropriate time and see for ourselves. That should clear up any misunderstanding, wouldn't you say, Phillipa? Miss Talbot?''

''Why, yes, Mama, what a splendid idea. And I shall

wear my new dress. The violet with the lace coquings on the sleeves.''

''Very well then.'' Lady Raynes beamed. ''It is settled.''

Lark bid her time until after Lady Raynes and Miss Phillipa had set out to make their morning calls. Even though they rarely returned before six, that still only gave Lark three hours to put her plan into motion.

Sneaking out of the house unnoticed presented very little challenge. The Rayneses' butler rarely exited the pantry. The housekeeper was always busy supervising her staff, ordering the housemaids to hurry up, stir the fire, bring up the hot water, empty the chamber pots, draw the curtains, scrub the floors, polish the grates, and a host of other duties Lark once swore she would never be forced to execute again.

Not even the coachman or groom noticed Lark when she hurried down the walk, turning south towards St. James, and not stopping until she reached Covent Garden.

At mid-afternoon, it was still a bit early for the ladies she was seeking to be fully out and about.

In the evenings, especially after the theaters let out, they came to the Strand and Haymarket by the hundreds, wandering into men's clubs and theater lobbies, soliciting customers.

It was an option Lark had briefly considered, following her resolve to escape both the squalor of life in the sewer and in a country-home kitchen. What stopped her were not any feelings of morality, but rather a feint memory of a woman Lark thought might have been her mother. She couldn't be sure. Her recollections of the years before the mudlarks were mostly sense oriented. She remembered the smells of the workhouse. The sweat of too many people crammed into too small a place, the mildewed dampness, and the gin on the breath of the woman who'd brought her there, then took her back, then left Lark on the street to fend for herself.

She'd always equated prostitution with that woman,

and, although a great many girls she'd grown up with now made their living in the world's oldest profession, Lark knew it was not the course for her.

Which didn't, of course, imply a reluctance on Lark's part to employ some of the women for her own purposes. As long as she paid the set rate for their time, most of the girls didn't care what they were being hired to do.

May, for instance, did not even so much as blink when Lark outlined her assignment for the evening. She'd worked for Lark before, and all May wanted to know was when and where she'd be collecting her fee.

"You'll get your money when the job is done," Lark said. "And when it's done right."

"Nothing to it." May splashed a handful of water on her chemise, and tugged at the frock, forcing her bosom even more to the surface. "He's a man, ain't he?"

"Yes, but he's a very clever man. He's not like the others." Lark was as surprised by her words as May was to hear them. "I daresay, I've never met anyone like him before."

May cackled gleefully. "Maybe you'd prefer it to be doing my job yourself then."

"No!" Lark couldn't understand where the intensity of her denial came from. The word ripped out of her mouth without permission from Lark, and that absolutely terrified her.

The only constant she'd even been able to count on was her self-control. The thought that, even from a distance, Damian Moxley had somehow managed to destroy that resolve was enough to send shivers down Lark's spine.

"No," she repeated, calmer now. "You do what you have to do, and I shall do what I have to do. And, with a little luck, neither one of us will ever need to see Mr. Moxley again."

*   *   *

Lark was back at the Raynes' home in plenty of time to greet Lady Raynes and Phillipa when they returned from their calls.

Without even taking a moment for dinner, Phillipa ordered Lark into the carriage, announcing that they were heading for Damian's immediately, so that they might prove, once and for all, Lark's deception. Lark did not argue.

She climbed in meekly, accepting Phillipa's daggers-and-poison glare head-on, and refusing to say a single word for the duration of the ride. Across from her, Phillipa and her mother exchanged whispers behind cupped hands. Lark could make out her name and Damian's, but pretended to be too engrossed in the passing scenery to notice what was taking place only inches away.

They arrived at the factory just as Damian's workers were leaving for the day. The men brushed by them deferentially, some tipping their hats, others merely hurrying away, eyes downcast.

Phillipa watched them distastefully, their calloused hands and dirt encrusted fingernails reminding her of how little distance there actually was between these common laborers and her Damian.

It was much easier for Phillipa to push Damian's lack of a fine family to the back of her mind whilst he sat in the Raynes' parlor in his neatly pressed linen shirt, stock, cravat, breeches, and navy waistcoat with silver buttons, than when she was forced to imagine him spending all day surrounded by men in loose grey work shirts and pants tied up with a bit of rope rather than a belt.

The three women entered through the store, and when the clerk nervously offered to fetch Mr. Moxley, Lady Raynes waved him aside with an imperial toss of the hand. Someday, Lark promised herself, someday when she had finally made enough money to retire to a life of leisure as a great lady, she too would be able to sweep past people without a word.

Phillipa and Lark followed Lady Raynes up the stairs, towards Damian's office, all of them holding up their skirts with one hand so as not to trip. As they ascended, Lark took a moment to look down at the factory floor, noting the number of work stations. Damian probably employed up to one hundred people in his factory. She couldn't help but be impressed. What chimney boy wouldn't have given anything, done anything, to find himself in such a position.

They paused at the top of the stairs. Lady Raynes raised one hand to knock on the door to Damian's office. And that was when the three of them heard it.

A voice.

A distinctively female voice telling Damian, "It's as I'm always saying, dearie, your fancy miss can't be knowing how to take care of you in the right way."

Lark snuck a look at Phillipa.

Miss Raynes' face blanched to the exact shade other young ladies spent nights praying and days powdering to achieve. If a color existed paler than white, Phillipa had discovered it. Her lips parted slightly, but no sound came out.

On the other side of the door, May was still talking on, describing in plain detail exactly what she intended to do for Damian, when she was suddenly cut off in mid-sentence.

Damian's voice thundered, echoing not only inside his office, but up and against the deserted factory walls. "I do not know who you are, young woman, but I am giving you exactly ten seconds to get off my property and out of my sight. In case you are not aware of it, my heart belongs to one woman, Phillipa Raynes. And you are not good enough to polish her shoes or even look in her direction."

The door swung open and Damian unexpectedly loomed in front of them, clutching May by the elbow.

"Phillipa," Damian exclaimed. "Lady Raynes." Then,

in a slightly different tone, ''Miss Talbot.'' His eyes bore into Lark with such force, she needed to grip the bannister to steady herself. ''What brings the three of you here at this hour?''

6

"It was Miss Talbot, this is all her doing." Phillipa rushed to answer Damian's question, grabbing his arm to reiterate her point. "You can't imagine the horrible things she accused you of."

"Miss Talbot?" Damian turned to look at Lark, eyes wide with seemingly sincere confusion. "I'm afraid I don't understand."

"She said there was a woman that you met after work before coming to see me. Oh, Damian, will you ever forgive me for doubting you?" Phillipa latched on even tighter to Damian's arm. Something about the sight of her pressing so tightly against him caused a most peculiar stirring in Lark's stomach.

But she didn't have the time to wonder about such things now. Not when Phillipa was so gleefully throwing her to the wolves.

"Miss Talbot said what? I'm afraid I don't understand."

"It is I who don't understand," Lady Raynes interrupted. "Miss Talbot informed us she had heard rumors of your meeting a woman after work. Unless I am truly going blind in my old age, this"—she indicated May—"is a woman."

Lark thanked God for Lady Raynes. There might even be an escape for her in this, after all.

"Mama, please! Did you not hear what Damian told her?"

"Indeed, I did. However, I would still like an explanation for what this young lady is doing here at the exact time Miss Talbot predicted her visiting."

Damian released his fierce grip on May's elbow and turned his attention to Lark. "It all seems rather convenient, doesn't it?"

Now there were three pairs of eyes, none of them friendly, boring into her.

Lark opened her mouth to speak, but Damian interrupted. "If I did not know better, I would think Miss Talbot was deliberately attempting to cast aspersions on my character."

She was in over her head, and both Lark and Damian knew it. It was Lark's word against his, and Lark could guess exactly who both Phillipa and Lady Raynes would believe.

Lark stammered. "It was—it was as I said, I swear it. I heard, I overheard the men from the factory, they were saying—"

"T'was me, miss." May turned to Phillipa and Lady Raynes, talking so quickly it proved a hardship just to untangle her words into their proper order. "I was boasting, you see, just talking taradiddle the way that I sometimes do, making things up. I told the boys I was a special friend of Mr. Moxley's. Never met him before in my life. But I wanted them to look at me better, show some respect. I told them, and they believed me, and that's what Miss Talbot here overheard. I done come today to try and make things, you know, true like. But it wasn't, I swear it. It was all my doing. My bag o'moonshine lies."

Lark flashed May a grateful look.

"Well, there you have it," Lady Raynes exhaled in relief. She was so dreading the prospect of an unpleasant scene. Not to mention the laughingstock she would have been among her friends if word got out of Damian Moxley's preferring an uneducated tart to her beautiful Phillipa. "A simple misunderstanding."

Phillipa was still glaring from May to Lark, desperately searching for a hole in the two stories but coming up with nothing. Without her noticing it, Damian had gently untangled himself from her grip and was now looking at Lark.

To the casual eye, there was nothing different about him. But Lark could feel the rage boiling behind the calm facade. It washed over her like scalding oil, filling Lark's nose and mouth until she could barely breathe. Her skin prickled, raising goose-bumps along her arms and neck. More than anything, she wanted to turn and run from him, to just get away.

But Lark felt rooted to the spot, all strength drained out of her. She'd never reacted like this before. It just wasn't like Lark to fall apart upon threat of exposure. She had faced dozens of difficult situations before, and she'd handled them all without so much as a drop of perspiration. She couldn't understand what was happening to her. All Lark knew was that she didn't like it.

"Come, Miss Talbot." The ladies were leaving, and Lady Raynes beckoned for her to follow them down the steps.

Still slightly dazed from all that had transpired in the last few minutes, Lark took a step forward. And stumbled.

Damian's arm shot out instinctively to steady her.

He grabbed Lark under the shoulder, palm pressing against her side, four fingers barely brushing the softness of her breast.

It was the natural act of anyone, gentleman or stranger, upon seeing another fall. And the burst of heat that erupted from his hand and singed its way along Lark's body, may have been similarly natural. But she had yet to encounter its equal.

Lark gasped, covering her mouth with one hand, horrified that anyone, including Damian, might hear.

Damian, too, must have felt something odd in their encounter because in the next instant he yanked his arm back from her touch, slapping it against his side with a force severe enough to bruise.

Her hands trembled. She wanted to look at him, but Lark didn't dare. Not now.

What must Lady Raynes and Phillipa be thinking, witnessing such an intimate moment? How would she ever explain it?

Then, as if from a distance, Lark heard Lady Raynes ask, "Are you alright, Miss Talbot?"

Lark turned her head, looking down at the two women from the top of the stairs. Phillipa appeared bored, absently twirling her reticule chain around one finger. Lady Raynes merely seemed concerned. But neither showed any signs of having witnessed Lark and Damian's close encounter.

Puzzled, Lark looked to Damian. He met her gaze and politely smiled. "Good-evening, Miss Talbot."

Lark thought she was losing her mind.

Long after every other member of the household had gone to sleep, Lark was still lying in bed, playing the moment with Damian over and over in her head. Every time she thought about it, Lark relived the delicious flame that ran through her from Damian's touch.

But this had to stop.

It seemed that with every passing hour, Damian's power over her grew.

How could Lark carry out her plan under such circumstances? She needed to focus. She needed to keep a clear head. She couldn't allow thoughts of Damian Moxley to trip her up.

And then there was the fury in his eyes when he realized that the set-up with May was her doing. It was the same look he'd worn the night he threatened to snap her neck, and Lark felt convinced that, properly motivated, Damian was more than capable of carrying out his threat.

That afternoon, Lark had declared war on Damian Moxley. And he did not strike her as the sort of man to shy away from a fight.

With Damian gunning for her, Lark didn't feel safe. She couldn't risk spending any more time in his vicinity than was absolutely necessary.

There was no alternative.

Lark had to steal the diamond.

Tonight.

Lady Raynes had not been exaggerating when she told Lark she wore her ring at all times. The only times she removed it was to change frocks or slip on a spencer, since the diamond was too big to fit through a sleeve without the risk of tearing the delicate lace sewn around her cuff. She even slept in it. Lark heard Lady Raynes complaining about the awkwardness of it to her husband.

Lark sighed, and pushed off her blankets, moving across the room to open her trunk. Wrapped in a grey knitted shawl at the very bottom, lay a tiny bottle of sleeping potion brewed from a mixture of mandrake, henbane, opium, mulberry juice, and lettuce seed. She smiled. The rich could keep their doctors and surgeons. She'd take friends in the apothecary any day of the week.

Lark pulled on a dressing gown, slipping the elixir into one of her pockets along with a pair of handkerchiefs.

She crept to the door, pressing her ear against the wood and listening for stray footsteps. Convinced that the coast was clear, Lark tugged on the knob, opening the squeaking door a crack just wide enough for her to squeeze through, then closing it behind her.

Once out in the hallway, Lark crept towards the back stairs, wincing at every creaking floorboard. Her heart pounded against the inside of her chest, and, with each step she took, she felt as if someone were kicking her knees in from behind. She didn't dare light a candle, and so had to feel her way around in the dark.

Lord and Lady Raynes' bedroom stood at the end of the second floor hallway, directly above the drawing room on the first floor, and the ground floor kitchen. On an average day, Lark made the trip from her room to the bedroom to the drawing room at least a dozen times. It never took her longer than a few minutes.

Except that, on this night, the trip seemed to be taking forever. Lark shivered, wanting nothing more than to jut her hands out in front of a roaring fire.

She wondered what she would do if suddenly discovered wandering the house in the middle of the night. There existed no believable reason for her to even be thinking about this floor.

To go the distance between the stairs and the master bedroom door, Lark got down on all fours. With her weight more evenly distributed, there was less chance of a shrieking floorboard to give her away. The carpet rubbed roughly against her knees and palms, leaving imprints and bits of thread under the fingernails.

Dust rose to tickle her nose, forcing Lark to bite her lips to keep from sneezing. Her legs tangled in her nightgown, and she found it necessary to stop every few moments and kick herself free.

At the door to Lord and Lady Raynes' bedroom, Lark lay completely face down on the floor, before gently tapping it open. That way, if either the master or the mistress of the house awoke, they would not see a shadowy figure standing in the doorway. They might even think the door had swung open on its own, giving Lark enough time to roll out of sight.

Holding her breath, Lark slithered inside, still on her stomach, and crawled towards the bed. Lady Raynes occupied the right side beside her husband. She rested on her back. The hand boasting the diamond lay across her chest.

Lark kept crawling, pushing herself forward with her

toes, and using her elbows like boat oars. Her hair fell in her face, and Lark jerked her chin up trying to shake it loose. She could only imagine how foolish she looked. A fish twitching and dying for lack of water.

Finally she dragged herself parallel to Lady Raynes, and rolled over on her back.

Without raising her head, Lark felt around her pocket for the bottle of sleeping brew, unscrewed it, and moistened the handkerchief.

Keeping the cloth as far away from herself as possible, Lark took a deep breath of clean air, then sprung upright.

She pressed the handkerchief to Lady Raynes' face, ducking out of sight in case Lord Raynes awoke. She counted to ten, then slowly removed the tonic from Lady Raynes' nose. Lark's interest was in robbing the woman, not killing her.

Convinced that her ladyship was deeply asleep, Lark reached for her hand, and tugged gently at the ring.

Nothing.

Lark tugged harder.

Still nothing.

Any more pressure would rock the bed and risk waking Lord Raynes. Lark cursed silently.

She searched the room, seeking anything that might help to ease the ring off Lady Raynes' finger. Her eyes fell on a basin of water on the bureau and on a bar of soap lying by its side.

Rising to her knees, Lark steadied her nerves and reached across Lady Raynes to press the mandrake and henbane drenched handkerchief against her husband's nose. He coughed at the unfamiliar smell, and began to stir. Lark ducked under the bed, praying with all of her might that he wouldn't wake up.

After a few moments, the bed stopped creaking, and Lark felt confident enough to take another peek. Lord Raynes had rolled over on his stomach, sticking his head under the pillow so that only his mouth still protruded. There was no means for Lark to anesthetize him now.

She lay on the floor, wondering whether to give up and return to her room. But then Lark thought of Damian and how arrogant he had acted. Calling her an amateur. Lark couldn't let him get to the diamond first. She would show him. She'd make him see that Lark Talbot wasn't someone to be dismissed without a second glance.

Mind made up, Lark leapt to her feet, grabbed the soap, dipped her hands in the water basin, then ducked back down out of sight.

She rubbed her palms together, working up a good lather, then reached for Lady Raynes' finger.

Slowly, painstakingly, Lark worked at the gold band holding the diamond, inching it down towards her slippery hands. Soap dripped onto the bedspread, but she ignored it.

More.

More.

Just a little bit more, and then . . . finally!

The diamond lay in Lark's hands, covered in soap lather. She exhaled slowly, feeling as if she'd just given birth. A part of her wanted to laugh out loud. But Lark barely permitted herself a smile before she fell back to the floor, crawling towards the door and the hallway.

The next morning, Lark, along with the rest of the household, was awakened by the ear-splitting shrieks of Lady Raynes.

Lark looked up at the ceiling and smiled sleepily, thinking of Damian.

7

L ark slowly counted to ten before leaping out of bed, wrapping a dressing gown around her shoulders, and following the sound of Lady Raynes' screaming down the stairs and across the hall.

Servants jammed into the master bedroom, spilling out the doorway. The ones unfortunate enough to have drawn back row seats stood on their toes and craned their necks for a better view.

In the center of it all was Lady Raynes. Momentarily oblivious to the impropriety of the situation, she hadn't even bothered to change out of her nightgown, preferring instead to rip her bed to shreds, howling all the while.

Beside her, Lord Raynes tried impotently both to calm his wife and organize a thorough search of the bedchamber. Neither endeavor was showing much promise of success by the time Lark joined the gaggle of wide-eyed onlookers.

Miss Phillipa pushed her way through the crowd of servants, indiscriminately shoving and clawing at anyone who stood in her path. Lark had an elbow jammed against her ribs. The housemaid wasn't nearly as fortune. She received Miss Phillipa's blow directly in the face.

Once inside the bedroom, Phillipa's shrieking joined that of her mama's, as both tried to drown each other out in their calls for the Bow Street Runners, an immediate investigation of the premises, and for Lord Raynes to hurry on and do something about it.

Attempting to seize control of the situation, Lord Raynes dispatched various servants to search designated parts of the room, but their presence only added to the confusion.

Through it all, Lark attempted to keep a neutral face. She didn't dare appear indifferent, that could prove very suspicious. But it would do her no good to seem overly interested either. Look at the trouble sparked by her casual questions about Damian.

No, the best course of action for Lark was to try to blend into the woodwork. With any luck, she wouldn't even be noticed amidst all this chaos. After all, to the Rayneses she was just another servant. There was no reason for her to be singled out.

Except one.

Taking a pause from her sympathetic screaming, Phillipa looked across the dozens of heads milling about the bedroom, and focused in on Lark.

Their eyes met for a beat. Phillipa's brows furrowed like a pair of lethargic caterpillars. Lark ducked her gaze, then cursed herself for the stupidity. She should have met the questioning look head-on. Avoidance implied guilt.

"Mama." Phillipa's voice rose above the din. "Perhaps we had best embark on a thorough search of the entire house. Starting, I would think, with the servants' quarters."

Pleased to have finally regained some of his domestic authority, Lord Raynes dispatched a footman to fetch a Bow Street Runner detective, then divided the house into perimeters, assigning each servant an area to search, whilst he walked from post to post, supervising. Lark noted Lord Raynes had taken great care to insure that the area each staff member combed through was located as far as possible from his or her living quarters. She had to tip her professional hat to him on that one.

Her own assignment fell four stories below Lark's bedroom. It was a bit of irony that, after years of doing everything she could think of to escape, Lark should end up back in the kitchen, sifting through the scullerymaid's meager belongings.

No less than the butler had been ordered to dig about in Lark's room. Miss Phillipa's suggestion, of course.

A physician had been called to soothe Lady Raynes' nerves. But the mistress of the house refused his potions, preferring instead to bustle from servant to servant, anxiously inquiring as to their progress.

Within an hour, the footman returned, Bow Street Runner in tow. Accompanying them was Mr. Damian Moxley.

Lark heard his voice in the hall before she even saw him. And it vexed her to no end to admit that her initial, instinctive reaction was pleasure at the chance to see him again, instead of the more reasonable—and appropriate—suspicion. What in the world was Damian doing dropping by the Raynes' house at this hour of the morning?

He'd obviously heard about the diamond. Had he come to accuse Lark? To trap her? She shuddered and reminded herself to tread very carefully now that Damian was about.

Her most intelligent option, most likely, would be to avoid the man altogether.

A feat more easily said than done. Especially when she looked up from the scintillating task of sifting through jars of cleaning soda, to spy Damian standing in the kitchen doorway.

He raised an eyebrow at her situation, shaking his head in mock surprise and tsk-tsking his tongue against his front teeth.

"When the footman told me Miss Talbot was searching the kitchen, I had no idea of the depths you'd sunk to. My, how one does suffer for her craft."

Lark shrugged, turning her back to Damian and feigning fascination with cleaning soda. "Good-morning to you, Mr. Moxley. I believe Miss Phillipa is upstairs, comforting Lady Raynes in her hour of need."

She couldn't see him smirking, but she could hear it in his tone and feel it wrapping the air like an invisible, poisonous gas. "We are the only ones in the room, Lark. No one can overhear us. Would you kindly pause the humble servant girl dramatics and favor me with a few straight answers instead."

He tightened both hands on her shoulders and whipped Lark around so that they stood face to face, their noses only inches apart. At such close proximity, Lark felt certain he could hear her heart beating. Especially now that it had decided not to limit its residence merely to Lark's chest, but to diversify and establish pulsating franchises in the pit of her stomach, along her arms and legs, and especially against Lark's skull.

Damian's eyes bore into her, reaching inside Lark and wrapping tentacles around every throbbing point, urging each to beat faster and faster until the sound all but drowned out her thoughts.

Lark prayed for a moment to stop and collect her wits, but Damian was making that impossible. She could barely compose sentences articulate enough to keep him at bay, much less plan ahead for the inevitable tricks up his sleeve.

"You are the biggest fool I have ever met in the profession. You ought to be ashamed of yourself."

One part of Lark yearned to kick and scratch until she had wriggled out of his hold. But, for reasons she couldn't understand, and felt too frightened to verbalize, Lark stayed where she was, relishing the warmth Damian's hands radiated down her body.

He smelled of soap. And not the homemade sort boiled of lye either. Damian smelled of store-bought soap, the kind English gentlemen were required to pay tax for.

"If I am such a fool," Lark demanded, "then, tell me where the Raynes diamond is at this very moment. Not anywhere in your possession, I'd dare say."

"And I thank God for that."

"Why, Mr. Moxley." Lark smiled with pleasure at the

sound of her senses returning. Perhaps her previous attacks of deaf and dumb lightheadedness were less connected to the presence of Damian and more due to some rare, undiagnosed disease. Perhaps they were merely an allergy to cleaning soda. The thought cheered her greatly. As soon as Lark finished her time at the Rayneses, she would forgo thrift and spend the money for a visit with an actual doctor. No more surgeons, or, God forbid, apothecaries, for her. After all, soon, Lark would be richer than she'd ever dreamed of.

Buoyed by the idea, she teased Damian. "Have you found religion and decided to abandon your life of crime in favor of good works and alms for the poor?"

"I am the poor," Damian told Lark with a straight face.

She knew exactly what he meant. No matter how nice her clothes or how fine the surroundings, Lark could never completely stop thinking of herself as the filth-drenched, skinny mudlark scrounging for bones and nails along the bottom of the Thames. She wondered if, when Damian passed by the ornate mirrors manufactured in his own factory, the reflections he saw staring back at him were those of a terrified chimney boy covered head to toe in soot.

"I warned you, Miss Talbot. London is my territory. I won't stand for interlopers."

"Then I'd suggest you sit down, Mr. Moxley. Because, like it or not, you've lost. And I've won."

Lark knew she'd gone too far the moment those last three words were out of her mouth. Damian's grip on her shoulders tightened, and Lark feared he might be setting to shake the life right out of her. She tried squeezing out of his grasp, but Damian yanked Lark to him, pressing her against his chest and pinning her still.

"You listen to me," Damian's mouth hovered above Lark's ear. "Our business is far from over. You think you've won? You haven't won a thing. I am going to stop you, Lark. And then, I intend to bury you."

"Damian?" Phillipa's voice wedging in from the hallway prompted both him and Lark to spring apart. She turned back to the cleaning soda, sifting furiously until the air around her had turned into a low-flying white cloud.

Damian, in three long strides, crossed the length of the kitchen and stood at the door, opening it before Phillipa had the chance and greeting her in an overly buoyant tone.

"There you are." There was something peculiar in Phillipa's tone. She was ostensibly speaking to Damian, yet every word seemed directed over his head and in Lark's direction, like an amateur attempt at a sotto voice stage whisper. "I just know that you shall be the one to help us resolve this horrendous crime. Gentlemen of your sort are ever so good with such matters."

Lark did not need to turn around to see Damian stiffen at Phillipa's words. Even with her back to them, it were as if Lark could feel Damian's actions. And that feeling formed a picture in her mind. She sensed the affront Damian took to Phillipa's off-handed comment, as well as his struggle to hide it. Her cheeks flushed in sympathetic fury.

Why was it that no matter how much money Damian earned, how well he dressed, or how polished and mannered he became, he would always be "a gentleman of your sort" among the upper classes?

Oblivious to the insult she'd just slapped on her almost-intended, Phillipa blathered on, "Have you learned . . . anything?" The last word could not have more obviously been aimed at Lark, if Phillipa had grabbed one of the soup ladles and knocked her on the forehead with it.

"Not quite yet." To Damian's credit, it was impossible to hear his rancor in the cool of his voice. "But I do have an idea for how we might get to the bottom of this matter." He turned to Lark. "Miss Talbot, would you kindly accompany Miss Raynes and myself upstairs to Lord and Lady Raynes' bedchamber. I believe that your presence might prove invaluable in our search."

The sheer impropriety of Damian Moxley standing in Lord and Lady Raynes' bed-chamber in the middle of the morning only lent further credence to how truly distraught the entire family was about the missing diamond.

Lady Raynes had dressed hurriedly, as evidenced by the one button missed in back of her frock, and the loose strands of hair dangling from the quickly rolled bun atop her head.

Miss Phillipa, while apparently equally ready to swoon, had, nevertheless, remembered Damian's arrival. She wore a white muslin frock, cinched just under the breasts, and no stays under the chemise.

Lark hovered against the door-frame, hoping to render herself invisible, and wondering what Damian could possibly be planning. For the moment, he appeared in deep conference with Lord Raynes, assuring him that while a Bow Street Runner was a fine place to start an investigation, God helped those who helped themselves. There would be no harm in the family doing some detective work of their own.

Damian suggested, "Perhaps it would prove wise to retrace Lady Raynes' steps of the previous day. We might locate a clue as to the identity of your thief, and the manner in which he—or she—" Lark could have sworn Damian tossed that last bit in for Phillipa's benefit—"acquired your lovely ring."

"Why, that's a splendid idea. Do you not think so, Mama?"

"I suppose if Mr. Moxley believes it is worth trying . . ."

"Miss Talbot," Damian turned to Lark and her heart jumped into her throat. She looked up at him, swallowing hard, and waited for the inevitable accusation. But Damian only said, "Would you be so kind as to help us recreate Lady Raynes' activities. Run and fetch yesterday's calling cards. We will begin there."

Lark wished she could save Damian the effort, and herself the boredom, by shouting out that Lady Raynes' activities yesterday had unfolded exactly the same as the day before that, and the day before that, and so on and so on since her presentation at Court. She rose at nine-thirty, calling for the French girl to help with her clothes and hair.

Damian asked, "Could your maid have taken the diamond during an occasion when you removed your ring, Lady Raynes?"

"Absolutely not. What sort of a fool do you take me for, Mr. Moxley? I am very careful about such things. I do not even let Jeannette hold the ring while I am putting on my gown. I set it on the table, where I might keep an eye on it. And then I promptly slip it back onto my finger."

"Furthermore," Phillipa chimed in, "how could Jeanette both help Mama with her frocks and steal the ring? Her hands are always much too busy."

Damian nodded. "So we eliminate Jeanette as a possibility. Miss Talbot, please make a note of that."

Breakfast, ham and eggs followed by tarts and tea, was served promptly at ten-thirty. After breakfast, Lady Raynes retired to the sitting room to attend to her correspondence and delegate the lesser duties to Lark.

Damian asked, "And did you ever during that time remove your ring for any reason?"

"What reason might there be?"

"Mama?" Phillipa's eyes darted briefly to Lark, and she phrased her question very carefully. "Did you not tell me once that your hand grew weary, writing?"

"Indeed. But thank goodness for Miss Talbot. Her assistance has proven invaluable to me."

"Yes," Phillipa said. "Thank goodness for Miss Talbot."

The guests came calling between three and six o'clock in the afternoon. They left their cards with the butler and waited to be told whether or not Lady Raynes was at home. Those informed that indeed she was, took the stairs to the first floor drawing room. They rarely stayed more than fifteen or twenty minutes, and their conversation mostly centered on the seemingly inexhaustible topic of the day's weather. Personally, Lark thought she might have gone mad being forced to exchange the same pleasantries over and over again during the course of the day. But both Lady Raynes and Miss Phillipa appeared to thoroughly enjoy the activity.

Smiling, Damian asked, "And I suppose that we can rule out any of your callers surreptitiously removing the ring whilst you were all momentarily looking elsewhere?"

Despite her frazzled condition, even Lady Raynes had to join her husband and daughter in laughing at the remark.

"Well, then." Damian folded both arms across his chest. "The obvious answer is that the diamond was removed while you slept. And, since the Bow Street Runner tells me that there is no sign of forced entry into the house, it must have been stolen by someone residing on the inside."

Lark dug her nails into both palms with such force, she tore at the scabs that had formed after her run-in with the broken lamp. Her breath caught in her throat, forming a moist, thick lump that refused to go up or down. She wanted to close her eyes, then open them again to find that Lady Raynes and her diamond and Miss Phillipa and especially Damian Moxley were all figments of some bizarre fever dream.

Damian was saying, "Most of the staff have served you for many years, have they not?"

"Except for Miss Talbot."

"Yes." Damian swiveled his head, facing Lark. The look in his eyes reminded her of the night lightning had first illuminated his features. "Except for Miss Talbot."

8

She wanted to pummel Damian with her fists, to slap his face until no trace of that smug, self-satisfied grin remained. She wanted to stand up and scream that he was as much a fraud as she, that he was playing them all for fools, that the Rayneses had more to fear from Damian than from Lark.

But, of course, she did none of those things.

The minute Lord and Lady Raynes and Miss Phillipa turned their accusatory gaze in her direction, Lark lifted her head, looking them straight in the eye and twisting her features into the most befuddled stance she was capable of.

Phillipa announced, "Of course. It had to be her. Before she arrived, we never had any problems with valuables disappearing in the middle of the night."

"Me?" Lark's voice came in a hoarse whisper. Her terror, most certainly, was not an act. "You think that I stole your ring?"

"Who else could it be?" Phillipa stood up, heading for the door and calling for the Bow Street Runner to hurry in and join them. "We've found the culprit, detective. She was right here in front of our noses all along."

Despite Lark's tearful protestations of innocence, Lady Raynes' hesitancy, and the Bow Street Runner's general's confusion, Phillipa insisted that Lark be immediately arrested. The officer had no choice but to comply.

They took her straight to the police magistrate at the Central Criminal Court in Old Bailey. Lark cursed her luck. All her previous experiences with the law had been with country parish constables. The unpaid locals with no police training were relatively easy to twist with a few tears, a sad story, and a play on the impropriety of making accusations against a lady.

But the Bow Street Runners were different. They worked on a fee and reward basis. And Lark could only imagine how much Lord Raynes had offered for the return of his wife's beloved diamond. They had a much greater stake in completing their job correctly.

And this was no minor crime. The law dictated a prisoner hung for stealing an item worth more than five shillings. Lark had yet to get a professional appraisal, but she suspected Lady Raynes' ring to weigh in at a good deal more than that. At least they could only kill her once. But, nevertheless, it was not one of Lark's goals to end this year dead and swinging, chained, from a gibbet, as a deterrent for other young ladies thinking about embarking on a life of thievery.

She knew her best opportunity for avoiding the hangman lay in first avoiding an appearance before the police magistrate. Once she stood in court, justice was notoriously swift. No jury was required, and with Lark not allowed to speak in her own behalf, only the Rayneses' accusation would be heard. And Damian's.

At the thought of his name, a pain so sharp she could barely stand cut through Lark's chest, as if she'd inhaled too deeply on a freezing winter day. She couldn't understand it. Lark should have been feeling furious with Damian. And she was. But she was also feeling betrayed. As if Damian had gone back on some unspoken promise between the two of them. Which was rather foolish, really, considering that the only promise he'd actually spoken out loud was his threat to bury Lark. Well, he certainly did his best.

Only Lark possessed no intention of letting him get away with it. Damian may have called Lark an unprofessional fool, but Lark knew better. She would have the last laugh after all.

While they waited for the police magistrate to call her case, the Bow Street Runner who'd arrested Lark locked her in a jail cell in the basement. The only light came from a window slit cut high up in the wall. The room smelled of rotted foods and unwashed bodies.

"You hold no case against me," Lark told the detective. It was true. There was nothing he could say to argue the point. Lark pressed, "I daresay, you will look rather foolish, marching into court without a shred of proof."

"Proving a crime's the magistrate's job, not mine, miss."

"But surely, he expects some bit of help in the matter. Why, you have not even found the diamond as of yet."

"We shall," the Runner insisted stubbornly.

But Lark could see her words were slowly inching their way into his brain. No one wanted to look a fool before the magistrate. And a detective dragging an alleged thief into court without proof took the risk of being laughed straight out of the profession.

Lark taunted, "Has a thorough search of my room turned up the missing jewel, or even a clue as to where I may have hidden it?"

"We are still searching."

"If I were in your shoes, I would refrain from making a case to the magistrate until I had at least unearthed some evidence." Lark sighed. "But I suppose you know your job better than I."

Damian came to see Lark a few hours after her arrest. She knew that he would. If Lark were in Damian's shoes, she wouldn't have been able to stay away.

She expected to see him euphoric. After all, everything

had happened exactly as he arranged it. If Damian had been merely smug before, he should be bursting his buttons with condescension now that Lark was in prison. Or, at least, that's what she assumed.

But the man who stood on the other side of the cast-iron bars from her was neither gloating nor pompous. He simply looked . . . tired. His shoulders hunched ever so slightly, and Damian's arms hung listlessly at his sides. He took a deep breath and ran his fingers through his hair, briefly resting the hand atop his head, as if unsure of what to do or say next.

Lark's first incomprehensible impulse was to apologize to him. Although she hadn't the faintest idea for what.

Softly, Damian said, "You did this to yourself. I warned you."

"I most certainly did not have myself arrested."

"You created a situation where I had no other choice."

"Oh? Well, then, I'll remember to shed a tear or two for you, Mr. Moxley, as I am led off to the gallows." She couldn't get over his cheek. Did Damian actually expect Lark to feel sorry for him?

His features hardened. "I gave you ample notice to stay out of my way. You chose to ignore me."

"And I am ignoring you still. What did you tell me earlier? That this was all far from over? Well, you didn't know how correct you were. This *is* very far from over. And when I get out of here, you will pay for everything that you've done to me. Everything."

A day long search of the Raynes' household failed to turn up either the diamond, or any evidence linking Lark to the theft.

Even Damian and Phillipa could not conceive of a suitable answer for how, if she really was the person responsible, Lark had managed to sneak in and out of the house without being heard, to hide the jewel elsewhere.

When Lord and Lady Raynes came to see Lark at the prison, they found no trace of the furious young woman who'd threatened Damian Moxley. Instead, in her place, was a quivering, sobbing Lark, swearing her innocence and begging for them to please, please, get her out of this horrid place.

Finally, Lady Raynes could stand it no longer. She ordered her husband to see that Lark was released immediately. They had no evidence of the girl's guilt, after all.

Her version of an apology was to tell Lark, "There, there, no harm done, my dear. Just another misunderstanding, wouldn't you say? All's well that ends well."

Lark feared that, after everything that had happened, she would be unable to return home upon being let out of prison. It wasn't so much that Lark missed the stacks of correspondence to address or Miss Phillipa's winning company, but that there was still work to be done, and an eviction would severely hinder her plans.

Fortunately, Lord Raynes was too frightened of what people might think if word got out that he'd dismissed Lark after falsely accusing her of theft, to do anything short of inviting Lark to resume both her position and residence.

Lady Raynes, worn out from the past twenty-four hours' events and still in deep mourning for the missing ring, seconded his invitation, and promptly retired to her bed.

Miss Phillipa, however, was less than ecstatic to see Lark walking back in through the Raynes front door.

"How could you, Papa?" She grabbed Lord Raynes by the arm and pulled him into a corner, exchanging furious hisses mixed with periodic glares in Lark's direction. "After what Damian said?"

"Mr. Moxley was merely hypothesizing. Attributing guilt to Miss Talbot was reasonable, albeit erroneous. I could not, in good conscience, allow the girl to remain in jail, Phillipa."

"Oh, what harm could a few more days have done?" Phillipa pouted like a child.

"I shall tell you what harm it would have done. If we were to insist on Miss Talbot remaining in jail, the magistrate would have considered our case solved. What motivation then would there have been for the detectives to continue their search for the truly guilty? After all, Phillipa, the most important matter in all of this is the recovery of your mother's ring.''

''I still think that Lark has it hidden somewhere. Perhaps there was an accomplice. A conspiracy.''

''My dear child, please.'' Lord Raynes waved the suggestion away as foolishness, patting Phillipa on the shoulder. ''Conspiracy requires complex planning, intelligence, attention to detail. What woman is capable of such things?'' He shook his head. ''No. It was folly from the start to even think a crime of such magnitude could have been committed by any woman, especially *that* simple girl.''

Lark sat in Lady Raynes' sitting room, dutifully sorting through the letters of introduction, *pour prendre conge* departure cards, and other correspondence accumulated during her absence, when Miss Phillipa entered and crossed to stand directly above Lark, glowering down at her.

''You may have fooled the detectives. But you do not fool me. I know you have Mama's ring hidden. And I intend to find it.''

''All the best to you then, Miss Phillipa.'' Lark could not help the sarcasm in her voice. ''Happy hunting.''

Miss Phillipa proved good at her word.

Convinced that Lark had the diamond hidden somewhere outside the Raynes' home, Phillipa ordered her own footman to follow Lark whenever she so much as stepped through the front door. He followed Lark as she picked up a hat for Lady Raynes on Bond Street. He followed her on an errand to buy more writing paper. By the end of the week, Lark grew so used to turning around and finding Miss Phillipa's footman in pursuit, that the one time he did not instantly appear she felt sincerely worried that something had happened to the poor man.

*   *   *

Lark had not seen Damian since the afternoon he had come to visit her in prison. Yet, she could not stop thinking about him.

Why had he seemed so upset? Surely, it could not have been the sight of Lark behind bars that threw him in such a state. Not when it had all been his doing.

Even now, she could imagine him lying in wait, biding his time until she made a mistake so that he could spring on her. Damian was determined to ultimately possess the Raynes diamond.

So that made two people, Damian and Miss Phillipa, watching her every move. Three, if one wished to count the footman.

And that was without the dozens of Bow Street Runners currently prowling London, peeking into each pawnshop, questioning every gem dealer, trying to find the diamond and its seller.

Lark had expected as much, of course. Did the police really think she would be stupid enough to steal the diamond one day and try to sell it the next? Lark had been in the business long enough to understand the importance of biding her time.

She would wait until the Raynes diamond was practically forgotten by all but the most immediate victims. Then, she would smuggle it to one of the colonies—Australia, India, maybe even America—and hunt about for the best price there.

The most difficult aspect of the plan was keeping the diamond under wraps until such time as she was ready to sell it. The last thing Lark wanted was to be caught with the gem in her possession.

That was why she had hidden it in a location destined to go unsearched for six, possibly nine more months. By then, Lark would have long made her escape.

Usually, once she had stashed her booty, she could go for as long as it took without giving into temptation and taking the risk of checking on its safety. But this job was

different. There were too many people aiming for her.
Lark couldn't feel complacent.

She knew it was dangerous, but Lark felt obligated to
look in on the diamond and make sure it were still safe
and sound. And she had to do it without being caught by
one of her many trackers.

At least she did not need to worry about Phillipa's footman or the Bow Street Runners. Their assigned area was
outside the Raynes' household, and Lark certainly would
have never chanced stashing her ring out there.

Inside the house, Lark only needed to avoid the
Raynes family and their servants. A not particularly difficult task, especially on those mornings when Lord
Raynes left early, and Lady Raynes and Miss Phillipa decided to go riding about in Hyde Park before nuncheon,
so that they might accept further condolences over the loss
of the family diamond.

Lark waited until the underhousemaids had finished ti-
dying up Lord and Lady Raynes' bedchamber, and the
upperhousemaids ceased their infernal flower arranging,
before creeping up to the third floor. She supposed Damian would have called her foolish for sneaking about in
the daytime, but it couldn't be helped. The compulsion to
know her diamond was where she had last left it was
keeping Lark up nights. It was making her anxious. And
anxious people often made foolish mistake.

Lark hoped that if she could just see the ring for herself,
it might calm her anxiety and she could stop fearing making a stupid error. Unless, of course, going to check on
the diamond was exactly the stupid error she so lived in
terror of making.

Once inside Lady Raynes' chamber, Lark opened the
door to the dressing room, hurrying past the spring frocks
hanging towards the front, and moved to the very back,
where Lady Raynes rotated her winter wardrobe as soon
as the last of the snow melted.

There, among the long-sleeved gowns, fur-lined bonnets, and calf-high leather boots, hung Lady Raynes' ex-

tensive collection of heavy coats. Lark reached for the burgundy with a double-row of gold buttons down the front, sticking her hand in the left pocket.

Nothing.

Lark's heart skipped a beat, then resumed its pounding at three times the normal speed.

Nothing.

It was impossible. Lark had felt certain she'd hidden the ring in the burgundy coat. After all, when searching for a missing gem, who would think to look among the victim's own possessions?

But where was the ring?

Panicked, Lark dug her hands into the right pocket, nearly ripping the lining at the seam.

She calmed herself, insisting that maybe, in the dark, she'd only thought the coat was burgundy. Maybe she'd actually slipped the ring into a blue coat. Or a red one. Or the white.

Desperate, she burrowed through every coat on the rack, plus a half dozen tea gowns and even a hat box.

Gone. Lady Raynes' diamond ring was gone.

Stolen.

But Lark possessed a very good idea of who might have taken it.

9

L ark knocked on Lady Phillipa's bedchamber door, and entered without waiting to be invited. She reckoned after the all-out war Lady Raynes' daughter had recently declared on Lark, it would be downright hypocritical of her to pretend to observe good manners.

Phillipa was still in bed. She jumped when Lark entered, pulling the blanket up to her chin and demanding to know what Lark thought she was doing, barging in at such an ungodly hour.

"Now is that any way to speak to someone who's come to make your day a little bit easier?" Lark stood already dressed, coat draped over one arm, and holding her bonnet with the other hand. "I have merely stopped by to inform you that today my business calls for a visit to Mr. Moxley's establishment, to fetch an order I placed earlier. Best alert the footman. Oh, and this time, do give him better directions. I would hate for the poor soul to get lost again."

Despite the presence of Miss Phillipa's footman following close in her wake, Lark could not help but feel exhilarated as she set off on her walk to Damian's.

Morning had always been Lark's favorite part of the day. She loved the crisp invigorating air, the relative silence of the streets, the freshness of virgin sunlight glis-

76

tening off the still damp leaves and grass. But, most of all, Lark loved the knowledge that a new day meant a new chance.

Yesterday's mistakes were already forgotten and today stretched in front of her ripe with possibilities. Her horror of the afternoon previous, when she realized her ring was missing, now seemed a great deal less tragic.

After all, it weren't as if the gem were truly missing. Lark knew exactly who had it. And the knowledge that all she really needed to do was conceive of a way to retrieve it from Damian, filled her with a strength-revitalizing sense of purpose. Lark never minded a challenge. In fact, she thrived on them. Now that she knew exactly who was standing in the way of her goal, she was dying to begin attacking the obstacle head-on.

She attributed her buoyant mood to the rush of excitement she always felt as soon as she settled on her target. That was why Lark was so looking forward to seeing Damian again. What other reason could there be for it?

She couldn't wait to see the look on his face when Lark told him she knew he had stolen her diamond.

First, she would compliment him on his cleverness. Only a gentleman of superior intelligence could have guessed the location of the stolen ring, then managed to sneak it out of the Raynes' home without any of them being the wiser.

She would flatter his ego, pump him up a bit. Damian probably needed it desperately after the backhanded compliment Miss Phillipa slapped him with in the kitchen last week.

And then Lark would get her diamond back.

By any means necessary.

The clerk out front told Lark, ''Mr. Moxley said for you to go right on up to his office. He said that you already knew the way.''

Lark thanked him and ascended the staircase. She

paused at the top, remembering the charged instant when she had stumbled, and Damian reached out to steady her.

What exactly had happened that evening?

Lark still could not think of adequate words to apply to the occurrence. Why had she felt so light-headed? And why, for just an instant, had she prayed fervently that Damian might never let go of her arm?

It was all most peculiar. And distracting.

The last thing Lark needed on this particular occasion was to feel distracted by a past incident.

The door opened. Damian gestured for her to enter. Lark thought she caught a slight rise in his eyebrow when he noted the spot she was standing at. But he did not say a word.

He closed the door tightly behind them. In spite of herself, Lark felt a slight nervous twinge in her stomach.

She said, "This is most improper."

"What?" He appeared sincerely puzzled for a moment. Then, understanding dawned. "For goodness sake, Lark. My workers hardly spend their off hours fraternizing with the likes of Lord and Lady Raynes. You can't hardly believe they'll go running to them, tattling that Miss Talbot went unchaperoned into a room with a single man."

"Well, no, that does sound rather silly."

"And as for that blasted footman of Phillipa's outside, as far as he knows, you've simply stepped into the back room to pick up your order. What could be more natural than that?" Damian paused at the front of his desk, leaning against it in a half-sitting, half-standing position. "Unless . . ."

"Unless what?"

"Unless it is simply that you are afraid to be alone with me."

"Don't be daft." The words slipped out her mouth so quickly, Lark could not even recall thinking them. "Although, considering the first time we were alone together you threatened to strangle me, and the next time you announced your intention to bury me, perhaps I have sound reasons to fear you.''

''Yet you keep coming back. What is it you want this time?''

She smiled inwardly at how easy Damian was making things for her. The conversation could not have gone better if she'd written him a dramatic script to follow.

Lark said, ''I know you stole my diamond from its hiding place at the Rayneses'.''

Damian's expression did not change. Not even an eyelash flickered. He was much too good of a card player to show his hand this early in the match. Lark admired him for it. Even if it did make her own task more difficult.

''I haven't the slightest idea what you are talking about, Lark. Although, I am amused by the proprietary tone you've chosen to adopt. I'm sure Lady Raynes would be very surprised to hear you refer to her treasure as ''your'' diamond.''

Impulsively, Lark took a step toward him. Then another, until they were standing nearly face to face.

Softly, she said, ''I don't care what it is you say, Damian. I know you were the one to steal my diamond. And you were so terribly clever about it. I don't think that I have ever met another man half as clever as you.''

Did he know what she was doing? Could he tell? Sometimes Lark suspected that Damian could see right through her. Might this be one of those times? After all, if, as with the other day in the kitchen, Lark had believed herself capable of reading Damian's thoughts, could not the odd connection work both ways?

At least he wasn't pushing her away. Lark wasn't certain if she could bear his rejecting her advances, false though they were.

Yet another odd impulse to ponder.

Standing so near to him, she could not help but notice that Damian's eyes were neither green nor brown as she'd previously assumed, but rather a most intriguing combination of the two. Lark exclaimed, ''Why, you have an

entire forest in your eyes.'' And instantly regretted it.
Damian was probably vain about his appearance. And she
had hardly paid him a compliment.

Much to her surprise, Damian laughed as well. His
breath felt warm against her cheeks. ''A forest? I've never
thought of it that way. But yes, I suppose that's exactly
what it is.''

She couldn't believe it, but he seemed to be genuinely
smiling at her. Bolstered by the reaction, Lark met Damian's gaze.

How easy it would be, to lose herself in that forest.
Easy, and extremely dangerous. And yet, she could not
look away.

''You are a most intriguing man, Damian Moxley.''

''I do my best, Miss Talbot.''

Gradually, his head inched downward, closer to hers.
Without meaning to, Lark felt herself rising on tiptoe.

''Everyone else, they're not like us.'' She was whispering, without the faintest idea of why.

''Thank goodness for that.'' Damian's tone was equally
hushed.

''Whatever do you m—'' Lark began, but, all of a sudden, Damian's mouth was pressed against hers and any
thoughts she might have been trying to formulate melted
from Lark's head like sugar in boiling water.

She responded without thinking, wrapping her arms
about Damian's neck in the same instant that she felt both
his hands settling on her shoulders. The feel of his lips
pierced straight through, as if Damian were simultaneously everywhere around her, before her, beside her,
outside her. Inside her.

She couldn't breathe, and yet she didn't want to. She
couldn't move, but truly did not care if she ever moved
again.

Damian's hands tightened their grip on her shoulders,
pulling Lark closer. Then, abruptly, he jerked her backwards and away from him, until he was holding Lark at
arm's length.

Her head spun. Lark's lips felt heavy and swollen, her tongue sluggish and lazily reluctant to form a sound. She looked up at Damian, yellow lights flashing in front of her eyes, as if she'd gotten up too fast. She couldn't say a word.

Deliberately, lest Lark miss a second of his actions, Damian kept her at safe distance with his left hand while, with his right, he slowly wiped his mouth with the back of one sleeve.

"Are we finished, Miss Talbot? Or are there more acts in this little comedy you've come to play out?"

It was imperative that Lark gain control of herself. She could not let Damian see how his kiss had affected her.

Mustering every last ounce of courage and control available to her at such short notice, Lark took a deep breath, clearing her head. "If you knew it was all an act from the start, why then did you play along so enthusiastically?"

"I was curious. How far would you be willing to go with it?"

"Do not flatter yourself, Mr. Moxley. The end point would have been the same whether you broke it off or not."

He pinched Lark's cheek. She ducked her head out of reach and winced, less from the pain and more from humiliation in the face of his patronizing attitude. "You have a great deal more to learn about the world, Lark. A great deal more."

"I know enough, thank you." Waves of anger washed over and superseded any other emotions, pleasant or otherwise, she may have been entertaining. "I knew enough to snatch the Raynes diamond before you could get your hands on it, didn't I?"

"Correct me if I am wrong, but did this entire farce not begin with a mention that the said diamond seems to have gone missing?"

"You have it. You have it, and I want it back."

She could still hear Damian's raucous laughter as Lark

stormed out of the factory and halfway down the street, Phillipa's footman dutifully following in the shadows.

Lark spent the remainder of her day helping out Lady Raynes, and keeping her anger in check. It rose every few minutes like bitter bile in the back of her throat, forcing Lark to swallow it down through sheer force of will.

The nerve of that man! The sheer audacity! The least he could do was admit he'd stolen her diamond. That would be the gentlemanly way to handle the situation.

Obviously, Damian Moxley was no gentleman. No matter how well he dressed or how fine he smelled or how many factories he owned.

A common street arab, that's what he was. No different than the grime-encrusted boys sweeping walkways or chasing rats down sewage drenched alleys. Lark wondered what ever possessed her to think him a gentleman of intelligence.

It was a good thing she'd learned the truth about him when she did. And it was a doubly good thing that their kiss earlier in the day had been nothing but play-acting.

Yes, that was a very good thing indeed.

Lark returned to her room after dinner, exhausted and looking forward to a long night's rest, followed by a brand new morning.

She was reaching for her nightgown, when an odd flash of light from the writing desk in the corner caught her attention.

She stepped towards it for a closer look, and gasped, covering her mouth with both hands.

There, in plain view for anyone at all to see, lay Lady Raynes' diamond ring.

Lark reached for the gem tentatively, frightened it might prove a cruel illusion that dissolved upon touch. She slipped one finger into the golden band, reassured by the weight of the stone and its coolness against her flushed flesh.

In that instant, the door to Lark's room flew open, and

Miss Phillipa announced, "What a lovely idea you had, dispensing with the time-consuming tradition of knocking. I've found that you can learn all sorts of interesting things as a consequence."

10

There was no time to hide the diamond, or even to slide it off her finger. The best subterfuge Lark could conceive of in the instant that Phillipa barged into her room, was to twist the ring around, gem side toward her palm, so that only the gold band showed. She tried making a fist, but the diamond proved too large for that. Instead, Lark merely arranged her fingers in what she hoped to be a natural seeming semi-circle around the stone. And then she prayed for Phillipa not to notice.

Luckily, Lord and Lady Raynes' daughter was too busy feeling clever to pay attention to anything outside of herself. She smugly told Lark, "I know what it is you are attempting, and, I promise you right now, you shan't succeed at it."

Lark ordered herself to stay calm and not jump to any conclusions. Phillipa's words could not possibly mean what Lark feared they meant, so the best course of action for now would be to merely wait, and find out what in the world she was talking about. There would always be time to panic later.

Phillipa said, "You are deliberately attempting to vex me."

Lark only wished that were true. But the fact of the matter was, she had too much effort invested in this job to risk losing it all for the momentary satisfaction of deliberately tormenting Miss Phillipa. It didn't mean, of course, that she wouldn't have liked to do so.

Phillipa continued, "Getting my footman to follow you to Mr. Moxley's factory, then disappearing behind closed doors for nearly an hour. You lied about needing to fetch a purchase. I know you exited without a single item. And I know why."

Now, Lark thought, might be a good time to commence panicking.

"You are plotting to torment me," Phillipa said. "To force me into inferring all sorts of unpleasant things about you and Mr. Moxley, the way that you did that horrible afternoon, dragging Mama and me down to the factory, claiming him unfaithful."

Lark exhaled in relief, briefly closing her eyes. Thank goodness for self-centered people. Miss Phillipa Raynes could not conceive of a single reason for Lark to visit Damian's factory that did not pertain to her. Currently, Lark was content to let things remain that way. Anything that kept Phillipa far from discovering Lark's true motives was certainly fine with her.

Her fingers tightened about the ring, its finely polished edges leaving red creases in her skin. So far, Phillipa had been too busy flaunting her ever-so-clever conclusions to note much of anything else. But the euphoria could not last forever.

"Very well," Lark confessed, hanging her head in apparent shame. "You have found me out. It is true, I did not retrieve an order at Mr. Moxley's. But I did joyfully anticipate your reaction on the moment your footman relayed news of my morning activities."

Phillipa snapped both arms across her chest, sniffing imperiously, and tossing her head so that the precariously affixed hair-bun on top slid slightly towards the left.

Lark did the same. The activity served dual purposes. On the one hand, it provided Lark with a more convenient pose in which to hide the ring. She pressed the diamond tightly underneath one breast, and covered it with her elbow. On the other hand, it served to annoy Phillipa. While Lark knew it would be unwise to provoke Phillipa merely for the satisfaction of it, there were no rules against accepting annoyance as the fringe benefit of a more productive action.

"I won't stand for this, Miss Talbot. From now on, I simply will not allow you the use of my footman any longer. There are too many other important duties for him to attend to, rather than to play the pawn in this silly game of yours."

Lark could barely contain her smile. "If you think it best, Miss Phillipa, who am I to disagree?"

Free at last from the footman's shadow, the next morning Lark wrapped the Raynes diamond in a pink linen handkerchief, hiding it at the bottom of her reticule, and set out for Damian's.

The workers at the factory no longer even registered surprise at the sight of Lark pushing her way past the store clerk and heading upstairs towards Damian's office. Lord only knew what they were thinking about the two of them. But Lark was presently too preoccupied with other matters to care.

Damian looked up from his paperwork when she entered. Was he pleased to see her? Lark couldn't tell. As far as she was concerned, the man possessed only one expression—infuriatingly neutral mixed with equal dashes of scorn and condescension.

"Tell me, Miss Talbot." Damian slipped his pen back into its inkwell and leaned back in his chair, looking up at her. "Have you no sense of societal propriety? I mean really. An unmarried woman visiting an unmarried man— and without so much as a chaperon or governess . . . it simply isn't done among the well bred."

He probably thought it funny, greeting Lark with the same protestations of etiquette he'd dismissed coming from her lips only a scant twenty-four hours earlier. But if he was trying to bait her into a pucker, Lark simply refused to rise to the occasion.

"Let us settle a few matters right now, Mr. Moxley." She tugged off her gloves, counting along on each finger as she spoke. "One, my visits are strictly business. Even the strongest of ton etiquette allows that a lady may call on a gentleman in matters of business. Two, as far as anyone knows, we are being chaperoned by a host of assorted workers inside your factory."

"It is good to note that you were listening yesterday."

"And three, neither I nor you can claim any pretensions of ever having been well bred."

Damian raised an eyebrow. "And what would you say, Miss Talbot, if I were to tell you that there is blue blood coursing through my veins right this very minute?"

"I would call you a liar."

He feigned being stabbed in the chest and mortally wounded. "I am deeply hurt by your conclusions."

"I beg your pardon."

"That's alright. I'm better now. I've learned to bounce back rather swiftly from rejection."

Lark smiled. "You'll have to excuse my incredulity. But exactly how many of London's chimney boys have blue blood coursing—you did say, coursing?—through their veins?"

"More than you might suspect," Damian answered seriously. "The titled are rarely particular about which beds they find themselves in at the end of an evening at the gambling clubs."

Lark acquiesced to his point. Even while living in the countryside, she'd been aware of the men's clubs on Pall Mall in Mayfair and St. James, not far from where May and her colleagues often plied their trade. Gentlemen who could afford to, spent days at a time at White's or Boodles, gambling away family fortunes in the false hope of acquiring someone else's. They most often played commerce as well as speculation, and vingt-et-un.

Lark frequently thought how much she might enjoy testing her skills and trying her luck at the clubs. After all, there was a limited amount of excitement to be drawn from such genteel card games as Cribbage or Quadrille or Pope Joan that were played by the ladies within the privacy of their homes.

But, then again, what did Lark need with the excitement of card games, when she was currently traipsing about London with the most sought-after diamond in England hidden in her reticule. For most people, that would prove enough adventure.

Lark asked Damian, "How did you do it? How did you return the ring to my room without anyone being the wiser?"

For a moment she wondered if Damian were going to continue playing the fool for her benefit. But he was apparently as tired of that charade as she. Damian said, "Paid one of my worker's boys to scurry up the ivy and pop in through your window."

"That's an awful risk you took. Trusting a strange boy. What if he were to abscond with it?"

"The child hadn't any idea of the trinket's value. Further, I gave his old man a job when the family had not a feather to fly with. The father would whip him to an inch of his life if he tried to rob me. Not to mention what I would do to him."

Again, Lark caught a glimpse of the ruthlessness that had served Damian so well in his climb toward power and respectability. She had no doubt that he meant what he said about whipping the boy if necessary. What was more, she felt confident the boy had no doubts Damian meant what he said.

"You intended for me to be caught red-handed," she accused.

Damian cocked his head to one side and peered up at her in the same way a benevolent father might look at his slightly daft offspring. "My dear Lark, do you honestly believe that, if I had truly wished you caught, you would still be walking the streets freely as we speak?''

"You are not omnipotent, Mr. Moxley."

"No. But I am very motivated. Had I wanted to frame you straight up, I would have sent my little courier to the Raynes' door with a package for Miss Talbot. Do give me some credit.''

He was playing games with her again. Trying to keep Lark off balance and befuddled. It was like the afternoon he'd kissed her—or she'd kissed him—or—blast it! It was working. She couldn't think straight now to save her life.

"So why did you return my diamond, then?"

"To prove a point." Damian stood up and approached her. A part of Lark instinctively pulled back, while another part strained toward him. "It was foolish of you to so obviously snatch the diamond. Granted, the Bow Street detectives don't realize that you are the guilty party, but they are on the lookout. How do you plan to hock the most sought-after diamond in England without being turned in by a pawn-broker looking for easy reward money?''

"I will wait my time."

"Hell may freeze over first. Besides, you do not think it will look suspicious to flee the Raynes household with a sudden financial windfall at the same time the diamond goes up for sale?''

"No one will draw a connection between the two."

"Never hinge your entire alibi on the stupidity of others. It is too dangerous. They may prove smarter than you.''

"The only person I've ever met smarter than me is you," Lark blurted out impulsively, then wished she could suck the words right back in her mouth and swallow them.

The last thing she wanted to do was add even more fire to the raging inferno that was already Damian Moxley's ego. Besides, it was one thing for her to admire him, and quite another altogether for him to be aware of it.

Yet, instead of puffing up like a strutting peacock, Damian seemed truly touched by her words. Fleetingly, she wondered if anyone had ever previously complimented him in such a manner. After all, the bulk of his clever activity, by its very nature, required secrecy. Like her, he could never boast about his exploits to another living soul. It did tend to make one feel a bit lonely at times.

''Why, thank you, Miss Talbot.'' Damian's gaze met Lark's and he smiled. They were standing close enough to touch, and he was looking at her so intently and so kindly, Lark felt certain he was going to kiss her. She turned her face up to him, eyes already half-closed, lips slightly parted.

Damian leaned towards her, shutting out all other detail in the room save his features. Lark's heart hammered against her rib cage, echoing along her limbs and flesh. She wanted Damian to kiss her, there could be no denying of that any longer, and, as he moved closer and closer, Lark inhaled sharply, as if the force of her breath might pull him to her quicker.

His mouth only inches from hers, the warmth of Damian's breath caressed her face, filling Lark with a sense of his presence so strong, she doubted she might ever forget it.

He rested his hands along the exposed flesh just beneath her dress' long sleeves, rubbing his fingers gently along her palms, then sliding both hands upward towards Lark's neck. She bit her lip to keep from crying out.

Then, without warning, Damian stopped.

He pulled back from her, arms dropping to his sides, and turned away. He faced the desk, tightening both hands along the edge, and pressing his full weight against them, head dropping down until his chin practically touched his chest.

His actions had an affect on Lark equal to being slapped across the face without provocation.

Her first sense was a disappointment so profound, she might have been slammed along the head with a smith's heaviest hammer.

But her second sensation was one of pure anger.

She wanted to curse and scream, both at Damian for his evil taunting of her, and at herself for so easily falling under his spell. What in blazes was the matter with her? Lark was usually much more level-headed. Why in the world was she letting this horrid man pull all of her strings, without so much as putting up a fight?

The most important thing, Lark knew, was to never let Damian see how much all his manipulation affected her. Lark's only defense where he was concerned was to cling to her anger. To use it as a weapon against him. Bruskly, she demanded, "When you are finished with whatever it is you are doing, Mr. Moxley, might we get back to the discussion at hand?"

He still had not turned around to face her. But at the sound of Lark's words, Damian's head slowly returned to its upright position. He straightened his shoulders, stretching himself up to full height. He loosened his grip on the desk and sharply tugged at the hem of his jacket, banishing any wrinkles.

Damian swiveled his head, the tip of his chin brushing his right shoulder. "I have a proposition for you, Miss Talbot. A business proposition."

"I'd sooner go back to dragging the Thames than trust you."

"Don't worry. There will be no trust required." Damian turned around, sitting on the edge of his desk. He linked his fingers and tapped them against his thigh. "The simple fact of the matter is, we need each other."

Lark wasn't sure what he meant by that, and so kept quiet.

He elaborated. "Please believe me when I assure you that, as matters stand now, it would be impossible for either one of us to sell the Raynes ring for even a quarter of its market value.''

Lark challenged, ''Why should I believe you? You've never told me the truth about anything before.''

''Actually, I have. You just weren't listening. Furthermore, I implore that you accept as evidence of my sincerity, the fact that I returned the Raynes ring to your possession. Why would I have bothered taking such a risk, if I thought I could currently sell the treasure for adequate profit?''

''I don't know,'' she conceded, then stubbornly added, ''But I have no doubt it was to manipulate matters to your advantage.''

''Oh, certainly, you may harbor no doubts about that. However, if you stop pouting for a moment and listen to me, you might hear how I intend to turn things to both our advantage.''

''I am not pouting.''

''Then kindly return your chin to its proper place beneath your lower lip. An attractive girl should never deliberately mask her assets.'' Damian dropped the compliment and continued. ''The only way in which either one of us could sell the diamond without fear of discovery, is if no one ever realizes that it is missing.''

''Too late for that now, isn't it?''

''Not necessarily. The first thing you need to do, Lark, is to return the ring to Lady Raynes.''

''Are you a caper-witted nodcock, Moxley?'' For an instant, the refined young woman of present day crumbled, and a mudlark shrieked in her place.

''Please keep your voice down. I should hate to have any of my glass shattered by the intensity of your pitch,'' Damian said. ''If you return the ring, Lady Raynes will think that she had simply misplaced her precious gem, and the detectives will be called off. Knowing Lord Raynes, he will undoubtedly take the ring to an appraiser, to insure that it has not been damaged. The appraiser will reassure the family that all is well. As soon as that happens, you and I will switch the diamond with an exquisite glass duplicate—created right here in my own factory. No one need be the wiser. We can then sell the ring abroad and split the profits. Everyone will come out happy.''

Lark had to admit, there was a great deal of sense to his proposition. But she wondered, ''Why are you all of a sudden so terribly eager to be my partner? Especially after all the trouble you took to call me an inefficient amateur.''

''You are an amateur. But as long as you listen to everything I say and make no attempts to strike out on your own, we should be alright. The fact of it is, you have much better access to Lady Raynes' ring than I. It would look rather suspicious if, in the middle of a heart-racing game of Whist, I suddenly leapt across the table and attempted to rip the diamond off her finger.''

Had he read her mind again? Just a few moments ago, Lark had been thinking of how dull the Rayneses' evening card games were, and here was Damian, all but echoing her thoughts.

''So then, Miss Talbot. Do we strike a bargain?'' Damian stretched out his hand for her to shake. ''Partners?''

11

Damian's outstretched hand loomed before Lark like a red flag in front of an already ornery Spanish bull.

Logic dictated that it would make sense for her to accept his offer. Logic also dictated that it would make no sense at all.

Lark wished fervently that she could just split herself in half, become two people, as it were. In that way, one half would be free to accept Damian's professional offer, while the other could continue despising him on a purely personal level.

Otherwise, it was very difficult to go about despising someone, the sight of whom made every drop of blood in Lark's body clot and pulsate into a single heartbeat so strong it all but knocked her off-balance.

"Alright," she said. "I suppose there can be no harm in trying things your way, Mr. Moxley."

"Splendid."

But she was already thinking of when her earliest opportunity to double-cross Damian might be.

It was only fair, after all. She had no doubt her new-found partner was plotting the exact same thing.

* * *

In her wildest dreams, Lark never guessed that returning the stolen ring to Lady Raynes would prove more difficult than stealing it had been in the first place.

Considering early suspicions of her involvement, she couldn't very well just brazenly walk up and announce, "Why, look everyone, at what I have found." And slipping the ring back on Lady Raynes' finger in the middle of the night was not a valid option either.

The only thing left to do was to stash the diamond in a spot Lady Raynes might have reasonably left it. But it also needed to be a spot that the detectives and other well-meaning gem seekers could have conceivably overlooked.

Since the only time Lady Raynes ever removed her ring was while changing gowns, her dressing room was the obvious location.

Lark waited until both her mistress and Phillipa had departed for their afternoon calls, then snuck into the room, taking care to miss being noticed by the other servants.

The ring lay safely tucked against her ankle inside her shoe. It made walking painful, but it also lessened the risk of Lark being caught with the diamond in her hands.

She stood in the center of Lady Raynes' dressing room, hands on her hips, looking from the ottoman covered in pink-flowered fabric beneath the window, to the sette painted in identical pattern beside the fireplace. Her gaze settled on the mirror, its dressing table littered with jars of powder, combs, and hairpins stacked in groups of five. Lark took a step forward, staring at her reflection. Is this what Damian saw when he looked at her? He'd called her a pretty girl just that morning. But did he truly mean it, or were the words just another way of teasing her?

Lark brought her hand to her mouth, and traced the outline of her lips with one finger. What had Damian felt when he kissed her? Was it anything similar to the sensations that had swept through her, leaving Lark breathless?

Most odd, this man and woman business. So complicated. Not like the relative ease of burglary. In Lark's profession every act could be divided into two categories—safe or not safe. But what to file Damian Moxley under?

"Nonsense." Lark spoke out loud, hoping to impress a solid authority that merely thinking the word never could. "You are engaging in silly nonsense. Now hurry up and hide the diamond before the whole household finds you day-dreaming."

She sank to the floor and crawled underneath Lady Raynes' dressing table, feeling the carpet for out-of-the-ordinary lumps. She wished that the housekeeper didn't insist on always keeping the curtains drawn during the day to prevent the furniture fading. Lark could barely see anything.

She swept her hand this way and that, until her fingers finally closed around a bit of torn carpeting. She slid her thumb into the hole, and tugged, making the opening another inch larger.

Unbuttoning her shoe, Lark pulled out the ring, wincing and rubbing the quickly swelling bruise on her anklebone, then ducked back underneath the table. Operating solely on her sense of touch, Lark slipped the diamond into the hole she'd created, pushing it deep within the carpeting.

Satisfied, she climbed out, wiping her hands one against the other to shake loose the dust, and sighed contentedly. Now all that was left to do was wait for Lady Raynes to return home.

She waited until both mother and daughter were inside the dressing room, before knocking timidly on the door and asking if she might enter. There was a matter of importance that Lark simply had to discuss with them. Immediately.

Lady Raynes sat at her dressing table, arms folded primly before her, while the maid brushed her mistress' hair, dutifully counting each stroke out loud. Miss Phillipa reclined on the ottoman, sorting through a half dozen new bonnets bought earlier than afternoon on Regent Street.

"Yes, Miss Talbot, what is it?" Lady Raynes could only turn her head slightly, lest the maid loose her count.

"I'm begging your pardon for the interruption, ma'am." Lark stood at Lady Raynes' side, pen in one hand, a stack of cream colored stationery in the other, and presented it for her Ladyship to examine. "But if only you might take a look at the—"

The pen slipped out of Lark's fingers, rolling underneath the dressing table and out of sight.

"Oh, goodness, I am terribly sorry. Let me fetch that."

Lark fell to the floor, indifferent to her unladylike position and certain that, within minutes, not only her breech of etiquette, but her very reason for being in the room, would be forgotten.

She reached underneath the dressing table, making a great show of sweeping her hand back and forth in search of the missing pen.

She stopped abruptly, addressing herself to Lady Raynes' maid. "I say, Jeanette, what in the world is that horrible lump stuck underneath the carpet?"

"Lump?" The girl blinked, uncomprehendingly.

"I would be careful of it, my lady. Why, you might step on it one day and cut your foot right open. It does feel ever so sharp."

Curious, Lady Raynes stretched out her leg towards where Lark had indicated, and tentatively felt around with her toes. "There truly is something under there. Jeanette, run and fetch one of the maids. Miss Talbot is right. I could hurt myself."

The housemaid Trudy curtsied when she came in and, all sense of propriety aside, promptly dove under the dressing table. They could hear her rifling about, crying out once when she raised her head too high and smacked it against the bottom of the table.

Then, "Gor!" Trudy's voice was a combination shriek and prayer. She crawled out covered in dust, her eyes as

wide as gold pieces within a face that had blanched chalk
white.

Without a word, she unwrapped her fist and thrust her
hand towards Lady Raynes, the diamond lying face up in
her palm.

For a moment, nobody spoke. Miss Phillipa half-rose
from where she was sitting, swallowing hard in disbelief.
Jeanette crossed herself.

And Lady Raynes let out a shriek so loud that Lark,
recalling Damian's earlier comment, feared for the glass
windows.

The remainder of the evening passed in a happy blur,
with everyone in the household being summoned to re-
joice in the prodigal diamond's return. Neighbors, hearing
the commotion, flooded in through the front doors, and
were invited to stay for a celebration supper. Footmen
bearing the wonderful news were dispatched to spread the
word. Any minute, Lark expected a star to appear in the
east and three Wise Men to come bearing gifts.

She tried to keep as much out of sight as possible,
ducking her head meekly when an exuberant Lady Raynes
begged Lark's pardon for ever having thought her responsible for the ring's theft.

"Why, I might never have found it again, if it weren't
for you," she gushed, and patted Lark on the arm.

"Yes, Mama," Phillipa said. "What *would* we have
done if Miss Talbot had never washed up on our doorstep? I lay awake nights at times, just imagining the possibilities."

As he had done upon first buying the ring, Lord Raynes
announced that they simply must throw a ball, this one to
celebrate its recovery. Both Lady Raynes and Phillipa
thought it was a marvelous idea, and promptly dispatched
Lark to write out invitations.

When Damian heard of it, he told her, "The night of
the ball will be a perfect opportunity for you. Switch

rings, slip me the real one, and I shall have it on the market by morning.''

Lark had accompanied Lady Raynes on a shopping expedition to Damian's factory. They were looking for a new set of crystal goblets for the ball. While a salesman occupied Lady Raynes by showing her the available wares, Lark stood in back of the store with Damian, politely making conversation about the weather—or, at least, so it was supposed to appear.

"You're terribly confident, aren't you?"

He shrugged. "No sin in taking pride in one's work."

"How many times have you done this?"

"Enough, I assure you."

"Is this the most valuable item you've ever stolen?"

"In a single swipe, yes."

Lark nodded thoughtfully, the wheels in her head clicking at a painful pace. If she could just lull Damian into a false sense of security, then get him to confess something about his past, she might finally find herself holding the upper hand.

Lark still didn't trust Damian to keep his end of the bargain and split the profits from selling her diamond. She needed a bit of ammunition to hold over his head.

"What was your biggest success before this?" Lark asked, hoping she sounded merely curious, and a bit awestruck.

Damian took a moment before answering. He seemed to be considering the wisdom of telling the truth. Then, as if finally deciding it couldn't possibly do any harm, told Lark, "I filched an emerald and ruby Christmas necklace from around the neck of Lady Emily Chalom without her even noticing it was gone."

"I am afraid to ask how."

"Good." Damian smiled and, noticing that Lady Raynes was looking in their direction, waved. To Lark, he said, "Of course that wasn't my most difficult heist. Merely the most profitable. The most difficult was a silver tea set I acquired from the Earl of Shonrock. Seventeen pieces, you must admit, is a bit much to stuff inside a coat pocket.''

"Really?'' Lark said. "That is most fascinating to hear.''

The bulk of the next day, Lark spent helping Lady Raynes with writing invitations for the ball.

A week was hardly enough time to prepare for a gathering the size of which Lady Raynes expected, but she was determined to celebrate her reunion with the diamond as soon as possible. And Lady Raynes was willing to see to it that Lark worked as long and as hard as necessary to get the invitations out on time.

For almost six hours straight, Lark sat hunched over the desk, writing name after name on a stack of invitations that seemed to grow bigger every time she looked at it. It felt as if every member of the some 1,500 families that made up the ton were to be invited to the Raynes home. Where could they possibly put them all?

The muscles from her neck to her right shoulder throbbed every time Lark moved her hand to write a letter. Her eyes blurred, forcing Lark to keep blinking so that she might see anything. With every breath she took, she needed to remind herself why she was torturing herself like this. She thought of the diamond, and swore that it would all soon be over. It was the only way Lark could keep herself from tossing the entire stationery lot into the fire and storming out of the house.

Lady Raynes popped in to check on how Lark was doing every hour or so. She looked over the invitations, catching spots where Lark's lettering might have been a touch neater, and suggesting she might want to rewrite that particular card over.

In between, Lady Raynes chattered on about what sort of gown she'd be wearing, about the foods she was planning to serve, the wine, the decorations. Every word knocked against Lark's head like a woodpecker drilling a hole. She was only half-listening, until Lady Raynes mentioned all the important people she'd invited, and hoped no one had been left off the guest list.

Lark raised her head, realizing that she might never get a better opportunity to speak her piece, but treading carefully, testing Lady Raynes' reaction to each thought before moving onto the next one. "I sympathize with your worries, Lady Raynes. I recall an occasion, whilst I were still in the Duchess of Hayley's employ. She had invited a good number of persons up for a country home visit when, on the morning of, the duchess suddenly recalled that she had completely forgotten to issue an invitation to the Earl of Shonrock. Well, you can imagine her horror. A man so important shunned! It took months, I daresay, literally months, before he forgave her the oversight. And even then, I don't think he's ever extended an invitation in her direction since."

"How horrible," Lady Raynes gasped. "Why, I had no idea the earl would be so rigid."

"He does not let it be known publicly, my lady. If you ask him directly, I am sure he would claim the warmest of friendships with the duchess." Lark covered herself. "Unless, of course, he might be in a mood to deny knowing her at all."

"How scandalous. Still . . ." Lady Raynes eyed the stacks of invitations Lark was addressing. "I suppose there can be no harm in our extending him an invitation. After all, what's another earl for supper more or less?"

"I shall attend to the matter immediately, Lady Raynes." The pain in Lark's neck and shoulder disappeared as if through magic. This was one invitation she would be only too happy to address.

By the time every missive had been sent out, not only was the Earl of Shonrock on the Raynes' guest list, but Lady Emily Chalom, she of the emerald and ruby necklace, as well.

Lark could not wait to see Damian's face when he walked in through the door to see his past victims chatting with his future ones. With any luck, they might even expose Damian's nefarious activities to the Rayneses. That should be enough to make certain he was never allowed near Miss Phillipa again.

No. Lark corrected herself. That should be enough to make certain he was never allowed near the *diamond* again.

12

The invitations Lark literally sacrificed her right arm for announced that, come Saturday, April the ninth, Lord and Lady Raynes would be hosting an Evening Party, complete with dinner and dancing.

Within twenty-four hours of her dispatching the first notice, the positive responses began arriving. By the end of the day, Lark counted over two hundred promises to attend. Among them were Lady Emily Chalom and the Earl of Shonrock.

The morning of the ball, the Raynes' household trembled in frenzy. Housemaids crouched on their hands and knees, polishing the floor with bars of bee's wax.

On the first floor, a suite of rooms was opened and stocked with refreshments. For the older guests, Lady Raynes arranged a cardroom set aside, so that they might amuse themselves with loo or whist while the young people danced.

Supper was to be served in the ground floor dining room. The kitchen staff spent days cooking up near-cauldrons of turtle and Mulligatawny soup, and arranging a table-groaning display of silver plates heaped with saddle of mutton, lobster with Dutch sauce, salmon, roast beef, turbot surrounded by smelts, turkey poult, green goose, plovers' eggs in aspic, cucumber, lamb cutlets, quail, jellied eel, and, of course, the sweets, pineapple in cream and cherry-water ices.

Lord Raynes insisted on his finest sherry, hock, and port being set out for the occasion, and even agreed to a few bottles of claret and burgundy, for those who preferred such "thin, washy stuff" to a truly fine beverage.

The mandatory orchestra—cornet, piano, violin, and cello—was set up at the top of the ballroom, discreetly hidden behind ornamental shrubbery brought in especially for the gala.

Lark watched the massive preparations with a detached sense of amusement, and tried to keep out of everyone's way.

Lady Raynes was in a tizzy. She had earlier decided against hiring a master of ceremonies to help with the introductions, and now fretted that her choice had been the incorrect one. What if there proved to be not enough couples dancing? Oh, she would never hear the end of it from her friends.

Phillipa was in a tizzy as well. She had purchased three new gowns for the occasion, all of them white, but with varying necklines and sleeve lengths. She spent the bulk of her afternoon before the ball trying on each dress several times, making up her mind, then changing it amidst a flood of tears.

And it was into such confusion that Damian arrived, asking if he might be of any assistance before the ball officially began.

As soon as Lark heard the butler announce Damian's presence, she knew exactly why he was there. The false diamond. He'd promised Lark would have it before the festivities began, so that she might prepare to make the switch.

Lark stood at the top of the stairs, eavesdropping on Damian's conversation with Lady Raynes. She was calling him a sweet boy for offering to help, but, truly, everything was under control. Miss Phillipa was in her room that very minute, making herself extra beautiful for Mr. Moxley, so that he might feel proud to be seen with her that evening. Damian gallantly responded that he was always proud to be seen with Phillipa. Lark rolled her eyes.

Damian told Lady Raynes, "We finished your crystal goblets this morning, and I took the liberty of delivering them in person. However, I note that all of your staff is presently occupied. Mayhap"—he pretended only then to notice Lark lurking at the top of the stairs—"Miss Talbot might help me carry them in. They aren't very heavy, merely fragile. And, to be honest, I would prefer a woman's touch with such delicate items."

"Why, certainly," Lady Raynes concurred. "Anything you need, Mr. Moxley." She beckoned Lark to join them on the ground floor. "Miss Talbot, kindly follow Mr. Moxley outside to his carriage and help him deliver my wine glasses."

Lark said, "As you wish, Lady Raynes."

Damian's curricle stood at the curb in front of Lord and Lady Raynes' home, drawn by identical chestnut geldings.

Knowing the difficulty of finding a well-matched, high-quality pair of horses, as well as the extravagance of purchasing a carriage built to be pulled by a team of two when only one horse might have sufficed, Lark asked Damian, "You do enjoy flaunting your wealth, don't you?"

"What else have I to flaunt? My name? My social standing? My extracurricular work?"

"A curricle is nothing but a rich man's toy."

"Yes. But it is *my* toy."

Something about the way he said it triggered in Lark a feeling of profound sadness she could not explain. How many of the things that she called hers, truly were? What did she own, after all, that she hadn't begged, borrowed, stolen, or lied for?

Damian reached inside his carriage, ostensibly to pull out Lady Raynes' packages.

But when he withdrew his hand, his fist was tightly clenched, and he turned his back so that anyone looking from the house out onto the pavement would not be able to see what he held.

"I dare you to tell me its difference from the authentic one." Damian peeled back his fingers, presenting Lark with a diamond ring that, to all surface inspection, appeared to be the twin of Lady Raynes' pride and joy.

Lark gasped. "It's perfect." She turned it this way and that, looking for flaws. "Did you carve it?"

"I am in the glass trade, after all."

"You're an artist. A bloody artist."

Again, Lark thought she spotted splashes of genuine pleasure cross Damian's features. Did no one ever compliment this man except for her? But, then again, Lark thought, perhaps nobody ever complimented him on the things that he truly cared about.

"I'm glad you like it," Damian said. "Now all we need is for Lady Raynes to like it. In fact, she'd bloody better love it."

For just an instant, the self-controlled, polished gentleman of everyday life slipped away, and in his place stood Damian Moxley, a former chimney boy with enough strength to keep right on climbing, until he'd climbed up into London society. Lark teased, "What would the Rayneses think of you, using such common language?"

"What would they think of you?"

Their eyes met, and the two burst out laughing at the mental picture of Lord, Lady, and Phillipa Raynes' horrified faces.

When both had calmed a bit, Lark told Damian, "You know, you are not nearly as unpleasant as you pretend to be."

"Why, thank you, Miss Talbot. And may I say that you, too, are not half as dense and annoying as I previously judged."

Lark stuck her tongue out at him.

He laughed again. "Articulate as always."

Why couldn't he always be like this, Lark wondered. Why did, most of the time, he have to be so mean and horrid that she never knew whether to scratch his eyes out or tear his head off.

If Damian had only been so pleasant at the beginning, Lark might have been willing to share and work with him, instead of fighting him every step of the way. It would have been ever so much easier for both of them.

In fact, now that she gave it some more thought, Lark doubted her judgement in deciding to have Lady Emily and the Earl present at Lady Raynes' ball. What purpose would it serve, really, save making Damian uncomfortable?

Lark thought that perhaps she should warn him about the surprise guests coming. But in that moment, Damian's friendly demeanor evaporated as quickly as it had come, and he told Lark, "Now, don't do anything foolish tonight. Remember, the purpose of our switch is so that no one ever knows the diamond is missing. Don't let your ego stand in the way of our profits."

Lark's cheeks flushed scarlet. "How dare you? If there is any ego to be checked on this street, it is yours. You think that you know everything. That everything is under your control. Well, all I can say is: The walls are closing in around you, Damian. And you won't even see them coming, until it's too late to hide."

Lark was still fuming at Damian as she got ready for the ball. Despite Phillipa's objection, Lady Raynes had insisted that Lark must be allowed to attend—as an apology for that minor brouhaha over the missing diamond. It wasn't as if Lark were one of the common servants, after all.

Unlike Phillipa, now using a half jar of powder to cover the blotches under her eyes from an afternoon spent crying over which dress to wear, Lark's selection of gown was much simpler. She only owned one ball gown from her days with the Duchess of Hayley. The dress was white with sky-blue ruche trim along the skirt's hem, long sleeves and high neck. Lark knew it was a great deal more conservative than what the other young ladies would be wearing, but the last thing she wanted was to draw attention to herself.

Lark pulled her hair off her face and rolled it loosely atop her head, emphasizing her cheek-bones and large eyes. She owned no powder or other cosmetics, and so settled merely for pinching her cheeks and biting her lips to give them a healthy red glow.

Lark slipped on her white gloves, looking the final package over in the mirror and feeling pleased with the results. She was at least as pretty this evening as Miss Phillipa Raynes. Lark made a mental note to take care and not seem as if she were pouting. Damian said that it made her look unattractive.

As the final step in her preparations for the ball, Lark slipped the imitation diamond ring into a lace pocket sewn along the blue and white ribbon decorating her hair.

Now she was ready.

Lark only hoped, for his sake, that Damian could say the same.

By eight in the evening Lord and Lady Raynes and Phillipa were positioned in the ballroom, ready to greet their guests. Ladies in white gowns and gentlemen in black coats spilled into the house. They exchanged a few pleasantries with their hostess, then headed towards the ballroom. The first dance of the evening was to be the minuet, followed by a quadrille, and then some dozen gallops, waltzes, and polkas before supper. No one wanted to miss a single minute of the fun.

Damian arrived the mandatory fifteen minutes late, dressed in formal attire, black trousers, waistcoat and jacket, with white tie, shirt and gloves. For Lark, who'd never seen him decked out so like a Dandy, the sight was enough to momentarily root her to the spot. She could do no more than stare at the fine figure he cut.

She wondered what Damian would think of her appearance this evening, and Lark waited eagerly for him to look and notice her.

But Phillipa hardly gave him the chance. The moment he appeared, Miss Raynes attached herself like an African red ant to Damian's arm, and led him towards the dancing, whispering, "Mama said that I might be given the honor of beginning the ball, and, of course, you must dance the first minuet with me."

Lark watched the couple move among the other young people pairing up in anticipation of the first dance, and furiously thought *I hope all the wax from the overhead candelabra drips onto Phillipa's head in a solid cannon-ball.*

Lark took up position by the door, where she might be able to hear the name of every arrival. Within twenty minutes, she was rewarded with the presentation of her own personal guest of honor.

The Earl of Shonrock was a tall man of about five and fifty, with broad shoulders and a head full of extraordinarily thick, grey hair that made him seem even larger. His wife, on the other hand, barely reached up to the earl's chest, and seemed to be made solely of excess flesh. It hung from under her eyes, face, and neck like a befuddled gobbling turkey's.

Now that Lark knew Lord Shonrock was on the premises, her next order of business was to make Damian aware of this fact.

As unobtrusively as possible, Lark pushed her way through the crowd until she was at the threshold of the ballroom.

Once there, Lark pierced her eyes into the back of Damian's neck as he chatted with a group of Phillipa's friends, willing him to note her presence.

After a moment, Damian did just that, turning his head and meeting Lark's gaze. He raised a questioning eyebrow, wondering if something had gone wrong with their plan. Lark shook her head ever so slightly. Then, with a sly smile she couldn't seem to control, Lark directed

Damian's gaze across the room, towards where the Earl of Shonrock was debating the merits of various French champagnes with Lord Raynes.

If she had written the stage directions herself, Lark could not have gotten a better reaction from Damian. His eyes grew so large, she expected each eyelash to spring off from the strain. Damian's chin dropped a notch. Enough for Lark to see his tongue frantically whipping from side to side, like a trapped firefly in a child's jar. He forced his lips shut and swallowed hard. But it wasn't enough to prevent all the color draining away from Damian's face, replaced by a bluish tinge.

Summoning every ounce of self-control, Damian politely excused himself from the conversation and headed towards Lark.

He grabbed her by the wrist, twisting her arm until she cried out in pain, and pulled Lark into a quiet corner.

"What have you done? God in heaven, what have you done?"

She yanked her arm free and rubbed the bruises his fingers had left on her skin. "You were so set on exposing me. Let's see how you like the taste of your own medicine."

"I told you," Damian was the only person Lark knew who could still convey shouting while whispering. "I told you not to let your ego get in the way of our work. You've ruined everything."

"Not for me. The Earl of Shonrock holds nothing on me."

"I should terminate our deal right now. That would be a lesson to you."

"How?" Lark taunted. "How are you going to do that, Damian? I have the duplicate ring. You've got nothing."

"Damn you, you bloody little chit. Haven't you learned never to underestimate me by now?"

"I could say the same to you."

He wouldn't dare raise a hand to her in such a public

place, Lark knew that. But Damian certainly looked as if he wanted to.

For an instant, Lark even wondered whether he might not toss caution aside and slap her anyway, for the mere satisfaction of it.

He looked ready to do just that.

But that was before the Earl of Shonrock's towering figure appeared behind him, and the old man's voice boomed out. "Damian Moxley? What the devil are you doing here?"

13

Lark thought she had seen Damian at his angriest the night that he threatened to strangle her. But nothing prepared her for the look on his face as soon as he heard Lord Shonrock speak.

His eyes, which Lark had previously identified as the most enchanting combination of brown and green, grew a flaxen black, pupils swallowing irises in one fierce gulp. His breathing quickened, and the purplish vein running from Damian's chin down to his neck pulsed visibly through the pale skin.

Lark had expected to frighten Damian with Lord Shonrock's unannounced appearance. How was she to know that the earl's presence would enrage him so?

What would the Raynes' guests make of his extreme reaction?

Lark never received the chance to learn. For, in the instant that it took him to turn his head from her to the earl, Damian wrestled control of his features from the demons that gripped him.

When he faced Lord Shonrock, Damian's expression was neutral. He may not have been smiling, but neither did there remain a trace of the blinding fury that had once seized him.

"Lord Shonrock," Damian greeted the old man. Lark

felt certain she was the only one capable of discerning the slightest of trembles in his voice. "It is a pleasure to see you again, sir."

"Moving about in rather splendid circles these days, aren't you, Damian?" If the Earl of Shonrock were playing to humbug him, he could not have picked a more apt topic.

"Do not worry yourself, my lord. I have not, as of yet, forgotten my true place in the world."

She'd never heard Damian speak in such a manner, and the oddity of his tone frightened Lark. How could everyone else just stand about, continuing with their conversations and dancing away? Did they not see there was something peculiar afoot?

"Word comes you've made quite a success of that factory, boy. Glassworks, they say it is." Lord Shonrock raised his eyebrow in a hauntingly familiar gesture that Lark presently hadn't the time to identify. "I suppose you'll be expecting a letter of patent and a peerage before long. It can't be helped. They're granting them right and left in this day and age. A chancellor here, a lawyer there. Why, even the brewers are lapping up patents like so much swill. Cheer up, lad. You might be next in line for services to the crown. It would grant you a touch of respectability at last. And, in a few years, no one should even remember where you came from. After all, witness the second Baron of Alvanley. His father was no more than a politician, granted his letter a mere one year past the start of this century."

He was definitely taunting Damian, of that Lark had no more doubt. What she could not understand, was why Damian stood so accepting of the barbs. Obviously, he did not wish to make a scene on the Raynes' property, but the motives seemed to grow deeper than that. There was a terribly rehearsed cadence to Lord Shonrock's insults. Almost as if he were as practiced in ladling them out as Damian was to receiving them.

But it wasn't like Damian to shrivel without a fight. If

Lark knew anything about the man, it was that. Surely, he would have to say something in return. And quickly.

Lark's vindication arrived a moment later, when Damian moved past her to stand beside the earl and suggest, "Perhaps we might continue our discussion at another location?"

On the surface, Damian was all gentility and fine manners. But Lark could hear the underbelly of steel in his words, and she cheered it. Not only was it thrilling to hear Damian turn his acid-dipped tone on someone other than herself for a change, but, she had to admit, his temporary meekness in front of Lord Shonrock had rather unsettled Lark. This was not the Damian she knew. And like a gambler at a horse or dog race, she was rooting for her own bet to pull ahead of the pack and come out a winner.

So when Damian and the earl withdrew from the Raynes' dancing guests in search of more privacy, Lark naturally followed.

Or, rather, she ran ahead of them. There was only the library on the first floor where the men could feel certain they wouldn't be overheard. Lark gambled that Damian, with his knowledge of the house, would lead Lord Shonrock there, and she pushed her way through the crowd of guests to arrive in it first.

She reasoned that her actions were not in the slightest bit intrusive. After all, was not Lark responsible for the pair laying eyes on each other? If she did not possess the right to eavesdrop on their conversation, then who in God's name did?

Managing to beat Damian and the earl to the library, she hid behind the heavy purple damask drapes.

Damian all but slammed the door behind him, its reverberations practically shaking Lark out from behind her hiding spot. She needed to cling to the cloth with both hands to keep from falling into view.

"Say your piece, then." Damian's words finally acquired the combative tone Lark had so waited for in the hall.

"You lying, ungrateful little bastard. I must admit, I did scratch my head, wondering the reason behind Raynes' invitation. I finally decided he merely wanted the chance to flaunt that rock of his in front of new acquaintances. And Lady Shonrock was ever so eager to take a peek, so I acquiesced. Never in my wildest dreams did I suspect you to be behind it all."

Lark waited for Damian to implicate her in the deed, but he did not.

"Perhaps I was nostalgic for my childhood." Damian said, "After all, hardly anyone makes me sleep on the kitchen floor now."

"You got your bed as soon as you were big enough to earn your keep. What would the other servants have said about my showing a bit of favoritism in your direction?"

Damian tried to laugh, only it came out more like an anguished cry. It pierced straight through Lark, making her want to leap from behind her hiding place and cradle Damian in her arms until he never felt cause for such a sorrowful sound again.

"We had a bargain, Damian. I let you keep all the goods you stole from me—including that silver tea set that had been in Lady Shonrock's family for three generations—on the condition that I never had to see your sorry face again as long as I lived."

"What a truly magnanimous gesture," Damian's voice wallowed in a bitterness deeper than Lark had previously heard from him. "Tell me, Lord Shonrock, do you make the same offer to all your *sons*?"

"Only the bastards."

Lark had to clamp both hands across her mouth to keep from crying out in surprise.

So Damian hadn't been joking. When he talked of blue blood coursing through his veins, and titled noblemen who didn't care which bed they fell into after an evening at the gambling clubs, Damian had been speaking from experience.

"It has never failed to amaze me, Lord Shonrock, how

you always manage to saddle that word with the accusation that somehow the circumstances of my existence are my own fault.''

''And I suppose it is my fault as well that you've grown into a good for nothing thief?'' The earl snorted. ''Had I known that you were lurking about when the Raynes diamond first went missing, I would have felt no doubts telling him where to start searching.''

''The diamond,'' Damian's voice sliced sharp enough to cut glass, ''was found safe and sound.''

''No thanks to you, boy, of that I am certain.'' Lord Shonrock moved to the door. ''I shan't pretend that I understand your reasons for forcing another meeting between the two of us. But mind what I say to you now, Damian. Try anything of this sort again, and I will no longer be able to hold a civil tongue. You are a common criminal, and I can make certain that you are never received in any London home for the rest of your days.''

''To hell with you!'' Damian exploded, the self-control he struggled so hard to maintain shattering into a dozen pieces.

The earl slammed the door loudly behind him.

Lark froze in her spot behind the drapes, unsure of what to do next. She still heard Damian moving about the room. He scraped a chair against the floor and sat down hard, taking deep breaths and fighting to compose himself. Lark risked a quick peek around. There were tears brimming at the very edges of his eyelids.

Sympathy overwhelming any instinct for self-preservation, Lark inched out from behind the drapes, and softly said, ''Damian?''

He leapt to his feet in surprise, hurriedly rubbing his eyes with both hands to clear the tears, and exclaimed, ''Bloody hell!''

''I'm sorry,'' Lark stammered, unsure if she were apologizing for her eavesdropping, or expressing compassion over what she had heard. ''I truly am. Very sorry.''

Damian shrugged, too tired to fight or even care anymore. "Well, you got your wish, didn't you? You've finally got a bit of goods to hold over my head. And not just mine, either. What luck. Although I would recommend holding off on blackmailing the earl for at least a few weeks. Let him calm down a bit."

The thought had never occurred to Lark, and she was proud to say she only considered it for a split second before honestly telling Damian, "I wouldn't do that to you. It isn't fair."

"Ah, yes, I remember. You do have a penchant for playing fair. A lower class girl with upper class tastes and middle class morality. What a charming combination."

"Are you alright, Damian?"

"You mean after my little chat with Papa? Oh, yes. I'm fine. That wasn't the first such row in our history, although a man can always hope it shall be the last."

"He's never acknowledged you then?"

"The bastard son of a dairymaid who didn't even possess manners enough to survive childbirth and assume responsibility for her pup?" Damian laughed at the thought, then sobered quickly, as if unexpectedly woken from a dream. "He did love her though. My mother. At least so the household staff told me. I suppose he had to love someone. And God knows Lady Shonrock never fit the bill. Can you imagine a married couple spending entire evenings, hour upon hour at a time, sitting in complete silence? They hadn't a single word to say to each other. And the creative excuses both would conjure up to avoid spending any more time than absolutely necessary in each other's presence! No wonder he turned to my mother. Coming home was the most torturous portion of his day."

Lark remembered Damian's earlier vow never to find himself trapped in a loveless marriage, and kept silent.

He continued, "But to answer your original question: Oh, no, my dear Lark. He never acknowledged me. The Earl of Shonrock's sole bow to paternal obligation was to allow my being brought into the household and raised in the kitchen. He thought I might make him a fine page someday. If I ever learned to obey, that is. Any wonder that I ran away to London almost as soon as I could walk?''

"The chimney work?''

"Aye. I started with chimney work. Did my bit as a crossing sweeper, rat catcher, waterman, coal whipper, you name it, I've done it. Bet you didn't know I was a regular Renaissance man? And then one day I got to thinking. No chance of my ending up in the old earl's will once he sticks his spoon in the wall. I'd best hurry and fetch my inheritance whilst he was still alive.''

Lark guessed. "The silver tea set?''

"Among other things. He caught me, of course. But I intended for that. I wanted him to know who was stealing him blind.'' Damian laughed. "But don't you worry, Lark. I've long since outgrown that childish desire for recognition. These days, I prefer my robberies anonymous and undiscovered.''

Unconsciously, Lark's fingers moved to the false diamond's hiding place in her hair band.

He asked, "Is everything ready then?''

"Yes, Damian.''

"Splendid.''

He crossed the room in three quick strides, swooping down on Lark and gently cupping her chin in his hands. Damian's mouth was upon hers before she even had a chance to guess what he was doing, leaving her with no defense but to respond. And it was over so quickly that Lark could do nothing but stand there, lips still slightly parted from the kiss, and watch as Damian continued moving towards the door, all in one smooth motion.

He winked. "For luck.''

Lark waited a good ten minutes after Damian left the room, before she made her return entrance to the ball. The last thing she needed was for someone to see the pair of them together and presume all sorts of incorrect things.

Luckily, no one missed Lark during her absence. Yet

another fringe benefit to blending unobtrusively into the woodwork. She moved silently among the guests, squeezing her way past animated groups chattering clustered in the corners.

Deliberately, yet without seeming to follow any particular path, Lark made her way toward Lady Raynes. The diamond hidden in her hair ribbon grew heavier with every step, until it was hotly throbbing against Lark's skull. The nervous energy pumped through her veins in ominous counterpoint. This was the feeling she lived for, the sense of omnipotence that came with rolling the dice and risking it all. She wondered how other people survived without it?

Halfway to Lady Raynes, Lark spotted Damian out of the corner of her eye, and, instinctively, turned to look in his direction. He was waltzing with the lovely Lady Emily Chalom, she of the missing ruby and emerald Christmas necklace.

One glance at the intimate way Damian's left hand rested on her back, his thumb languidly massaging the flesh peeking over the low-cut rear of her rose-pink dress, told Lark everything she would ever need to know about the method Damian had used to switch her authentic necklace for an imitation, without her ladyship noticing.

Lark hated herself for the wave of jealousy that flooded her senses at the mental picture of Damian with Lady Emily.

And she was even more embarrassed when the next thought was paired with a sinful shiver of pleasure. *If I refuse to turn over the Raynes diamond to him, maybe Damian will feel forced to try the same tactic with me.*

Thankfully, the more reasonable portion of her addled brain instantly fired back. *He shan't find cause to try anything but homicide, lest you move your sorry self but quick, and snatch the real gem from Lady Raynes.*

So Lark straightened her spine, shoulders drawn back in full battle stance, and, chin set in determination, stepped forward to attempt exactly that.

14

In theory, Lark's task for the evening was very simple. Smile, nod, avoid having any food or wine spilled on her only formal gown, and, oh, yes, maneuver the most precious diamond in England off Lady Raynes' finger and replace it with a duplicate stone without anyone, ever, being the wiser.

How complicated could it be?

Lark watched Lady Raynes flit among her guests, stopping to add a word here, share a bit of gossip there. She really did look quite lovely in the robin's egg blue gown her seamstress had only finally finished hemming that morning. But, to be truthful, all of Lark's attention was focused solely on the diamond. It were as if every light in the room stood dimmed, except for a single candle flare directly underneath the ring.

Lark barely heard the buzz of conversation all around her, or the hard-working musicians pouring their souls out behind the obscuring shrubbery. She needed to maneuver Lady Raynes away from this crowd and into a more private area. But how?

Lark supposed she could always fabricate some excuse. But then what? As Damian had pointed out, a frontal attack could hardly be considered subtle.

Lark was still weighing her limited options when a

break in the dancing was announced, so that everyone might sit for supper.

A herd of wild hyenas wouldn't be able to steal Lady Raynes' attentions now. Not when her most nerve-wracking moment as hostess was imminent. Everyone would be looking to see if she had arranged her guests correctly. Lady Raynes had fretted about this moment for days.

But Lark had neither the time nor the interest at that moment, to follow how the actual pairing process might come off. All she knew was that, by a fascinating coincidence, Miss Phillipa happened to be dancing with Damian at the exact moment supper was announced, so that he was now obligated to escort her to the table.

Lark barely noticed her own escort into dinner, although she could only assume him to be some insignificant younger son of an even more insignificant baron or other lowly ranked nobleman. She gave him her arm and followed everyone else into the dining room.

The table stood covered with a damasked cloth, surrounded by the butler and two footmen. A many armed epegene dominated the center, sending fantastic, equally multi-limbed shadows to dance on the walls, and adding, according to Lady Raynes, "accent" to their affair. Once seated, most guests could barely see each other around the gargantuan candelabra. To Lark, it seemed to serve no purpose beyond sheer size. But, then again, everything in the room had been constructed to look as large and as heavy as possible.

Everyone took their seats. A footman circulated silently, offering a spot of wine to the men. Lady Raynes had been so determined that her servants be known far and wide for their quiet unobtrusiveness, that she not only had the dining room floor carpeted to prevent clacking footsteps, she even ordered non-creaking shoes for the butler and his entire staff.

Lark barely tasted the ham she was slowly slicing and sliding into her mouth, and it took all her remaining con-

centration to remember that peas were not to be eaten
straight off the knife, like in the countryside, but, as they
were in London, with a fork.

She watched Lady Raynes with one eye, and Damian
with the other. Everyone must have thought Lark positively cross-eyed.

Damian sat by Phillipa's side, pupils glazed over with
boredom. There was nothing worse than being forced to
sit about idle, feigning interest in mindless chit-chat,
whilst there was serious work to be done.

On several occasions, she saw Damian looking towards
Lord and Lady Shonrock, his expression unreadable to
anyone save Lark. Only she saw the carefully managed
fury raging behind seemingly neutral features. She wondered if Damian were envying the life he might have enjoyed, had he been born on the right side of the blanket.

Had that happened, he would have been a different person. Just as handsome, to be sure, but without the fire and
hunger she believed to be his most arresting feature. He
would have appeared more marriageable to the ton, but
far less appealing to Lark.

From her seat, Lady Raynes signaled to the butler that
it was now time to bring in the sweets. Instantly, a fleet
of servants appeared, balancing an array of platters loaded
with delicacies.

They came in a procession, from tallest to smallest,
each one setting his tray upon the table, then stepping
aside to allow the next attendant clear passage.

At the very end of the line, the youngest footman, a
boy of no more than fourteen, struggled underneath the
unwieldy weight of his platter. He fought to keep both
arms unflaggingly straight, trying to ignore the sharp pain
shooting across his shoulders, lest he unintentionally relax
and lose his grip. He rocked from one foot to the next,
letting first one side, then the other, assume the bulk of
the platter's weight.

Lark smiled to herself at the sight, and, without warning, stood up, darting across the room towards the boy,

indifferent to the astonished stares accompanying her flight.

"Be careful," she called. "I fear he is about to drop—"

Her shocking, headlong charge straight into him was the final straw necessary for the young footman to fumble his already tenuous clutch on the tray of desserts. The platter slid out of his hands, and as the boy leapt to save his chocolate meringues, he inadvertently jostled the servant in line before him, causing the innocent man to tumble straight into Lady Raynes.

Brown snowballs dripped from the bodice of Lady Raynes' gown, splattering to the floor in a trio of splashes. Those closest to the scene of the accident gasped, drawing the attention of other guests seated further up the table.

Lark leapt to apologize, dabbing at Lady Raynes' gown with her napkin, but only managing to make the stains worse.

"You clumsy, clumsy dolt," Lady Raynes pushed her away.

Lark didn't blame her one bit. So far, she'd dripped rainwater on the rug, broken a lamp, dropped her pen, and ruined a gown. She was beginning to grate on her own nerves.

"Please, I am ever so sorry." Lark repeated those words over and over again as she followed Lady Raynes from the dining room and towards the stairs.

The last thing she saw as the massive oak doors closed behind them was Damian, finally smiling.

Lark continued begging Lady Raynes' forgiveness all the way to her ladyship's dressing room. After the maid unbuttoned Lady Raynes' gown, Lark helped Lady Raynes step out of it.

And, when Lady Raynes slipped the diamond ring off her finger in order to fit her hand through her dress sleeve, Lark helped her set it carefully on the dressing table.

Lady Raynes and her maid turned their attention to the wardrobe, searching for another perfect gown to replace her ruined one. Lark made a pretense of trying to help, but Lady Raynes bade her to step away, lest she ruin another frock with her stupid clumsiness.

"Phillipa warned me against inviting the help to a ball. And such is the punishment I deserve for being charitable. Imagine, thinking that a girl of your sort might prove able to move among civilized people without creating a massive disturbance. How foolish of me. You can be sure that's a mistake I never intend to make again. A secretary at a ball. Maybe in the countryside, but, London? How could I have been so daft?"

To Lark's ears, the words echoing from Lady Raynes' closet were just meaningless noises in the background. She stood in front of the mirror, hurriedly pulling the ribbon from her hair and feeling for the false diamond.

She'd hidden it at the very top of the double ribbon, but, during the course of the evening, Lark's moving about had shaken it to the bottom, where it now sat, stuck and immobile.

She squeezed two fingers into the ribbon's opening, but it wasn't enough to reach the ring. She tried maneuvering her grip downward, but the space was too tight.

Lark cursed under her breath and yanked her hand free, tearing a good inch of ribbon along the seam. She made a second attempt, this time with only one finger, but still couldn't quite grasp the imitation gold band and diamond well enough to pull it free.

From the wardrobe, Lady Raynes' condemnation of Lark grew mixed with pauses to look over and choose a new gown. Selection had narrowed down to the forest green sarcenet or the silver grey silk. That meant that Lady Raynes might be returning to the main dressing area, where the mirror stood, at any second.

Using her left hand, Lark slowly inched the faux ring up her unbearably tight hair ribbon, until her right finger could just about crook over the edge and wrench it free.

Hurriedly, she tied the ribbon back into her hair, no longer concerned with how it might look before Damian's, or anyone else's, eyes. Everyone assembled downstairs already believed her the clumsiest thing on Earth. They might as well think her incapable of grooming, too.

She balanced Damian's ring, and Lady Raynes', in her left palm, marvelling at his fine craftsmanship. To the naked eye, it was indistinguishable from the real thing. The same grooves in the stone, the same angles, the same weight even. A masterpiece really. What a shame no one but the two of them would ever be able to appreciate Damian's genius.

And once again, in spite of the tension inherent to her situation, Lark could not stop her thoughts from turning to him.

She felt as if she could look straight down through the two levels that separated them, and see him on the ground floor below. Supper had ended by now, and the guests were filing back into the ballroom. The musicians were playing again, their opening mazurka snaking down the corridors and up the stairs, until it reached Lark, binding her to Damian as tightly as any rope might have.

In her mind's eye, she watched him taking Miss Phillipa by the elbow and leading her to the floor. Lark had no doubts Damian was a marvelous dancer. He excelled at anything he did without seeming to exert the slightest effort. His movements were so graceful and confident, floating almost, as if he were walking on an inch of air above the ground that was inaccessible to every other living being.

The thought—no, the knowledge—that Damian stood directly beneath her, filled Lark with an unfamiliar heat. Now she could see him dancing with Phillipa, his hands resting respectfully on her arm and back. But it wasn't Phillipa he was holding.

It was Lark.

The magical, musical cord that stretched invisibly from Damian to Lark made it possible for her to feel the warmth of his touch as it reached up past the oak floors and carpets between them.

What a shame that the man cared not one whit about her, except when it came to using Lark for their mutual financial benefit. But then again, Lark doubted she'd ever be able to live without a plot or two, at least every once in a while, to get her blood going.

She smiled down at the two rings, repeating in a whisper over and over again, "The right ring is real, the left one is not. Right one real, left one not. Right real, left not."

Otherwise, the two looked, weighed, and felt so identical, she might easily confuse one for the other, and wouldn't that prove an exercise without purpose?

Not to mention the fact that Damian would probably blast her mercilessly for the error. After he finished laughing, that is.

"Lark, are you listening to me?" Lady Raynes' toneless babble unexpectedly twisted into a sharp-point rebuke. "It is considered fine form, at least in my home, to respond when questioned."

Lark jumped, fingers instinctively wrapping around both rings as she hid her hand behind her back.

"I beg your pardon, Lady Raynes." She hadn't the vaguest notion what the older woman had been saying, and now struggled for a noncommittal response applicable to any situation. "I wasn't sure that you had finished speaking. I didn't wish to interrupt."

Lady Raynes sighed in audible disgust. "Well, I have. And I am waiting for an answer to my question."

Lark took a gamble. After all, she did have a one half chance of guessing and responding correctly. "Uhm . . . Yes?"

"Very well." Lady Raynes seemed most satisfied by Lark's reply. Then, to Jeanette, she said, "The green one it shall have to be, I suppose. The lesser of two evils and all that."

Realizing she had very little time left before her lady-ship returned, Lark withdrew her hand from behind her back, meaning to hurry and complete the substitution.

Except for one minor problem.

Lark could no longer tell which ring was which.

15

Well, they did look exactly alike, after all.

That was rather the purpose of it. The rings were identical. Except for the singular detail that one was a priceless diamond, and the other common glass.

Lark's heart beat loudly enough to drown out all other sound. She couldn't believe she had been so foolish. She wanted to kick herself for it.

Blast Damian. This was all his fault. If she hadn't grown so muddled thinking of him, she would have been able to keep her wits about her and finish the job right. This kind of lovesick mistake was exactly the sort she'd feared making from the very start.

But there was no time for recrimination. Lady Raynes' voice drew nearer as she ordered Jeanette to hurry and arrange the green gown for wearing. Knowing that she had only seconds left, Lark made a spontaneous decision.

Grabbing the ring she suspected to be Damian's imitation, she plunked it on the dressing table, in the exact spot where Lady Raynes had left her original.

The remaining, hopefully genuine, article, Lark stuffed in the ankle of her shoe. She heard Lady Raynes and Jeanette approaching, and hurriedly straightened back upright.

"Lark," Lady Raynes shrilled. "I thought I had ordered you to your room."

Ah. So that's what she'd mumbled whilst inside the closet. Good to know, finally.

"Yes, Lady Raynes." Lark bowed her head meekly, and shuffled out of the room, walking as naturally as she could, despite the sharp edged ring pressed against her anklebone. She'd surely find a blister in the spot by morning. A small price to pay, indeed.

Up in her room, Lark pulled out the ring, painfully rubbing her bruised flesh. She studied the diamond intently. Was it the real thing? Or had she just burned all her bridges behind her in a quest to snatch a useless imitation?

Furthermore, how was Lark supposed to get the ring to Damian, now that Lady Raynes had banished her from the ballroom? She couldn't very well march on down there in defiance of orders. That would look most strange indeed.

But as it turned out, she did not have to.

Twenty minutes or so later, Lark looked up in surprise, indescribably delighted to see Damian, and equally as frightened of what he might say or do once she confessed her potential mix-up.

"Yes?" He asked, eyes gleaming with an excitement distinctively missing all during his forced time at the ball.

"Yes," she said, holding out the ring for his inspection. Before Lark told him the whole story of her adventures with the two diamonds, she wanted a moment to bask in Damian's joy, and in the way he was beaming at her with approval.

"Beautiful," Damian said. "Just beautiful. I must admit, I was starting to worry as the evening wore on, and Lady Raynes continued drifting about, diamond and all. But you were lovely. The highlight of the evening, even if those silly fools downstairs hadn't the sense to see it."

Lark lapped up Damian's praise like a parched soldier

in the desert. Finally, she had done something right as far as he was concerned. Or so he thought for now, anyway.

Noticing Lark's uncharacteristically solemn demeanor, Damian asked, "What's wrong? You're not having second thoughts, are you? An attack of morality? Conscience?"

"Well," Lark conceded, verbalizing a qualm that periodically pricked at her conscience like a pebble trapped between shoe and stocking. "You must admit, what we did was not exactly very nice."

"So what? I'm not nice, you're not nice. Why should either one of us lose a wink of sleep over it? I dare you to tell me, Miss Talbot, who, among the charming set below us, is nice? Lord Shonrock? Miss Phillipa? Lady Emily?"

"I'm sure there is one decent soul among them, Damian."

"Oh, possibly. But, then again, we aren't robbing them. We are robbing the Raynes family." Damian sighed. "Listen to me, Lark. If you want me to tell you that we are justified in what we are doing because Lord Raynes is a horrible sort who mistreats his servants and exploits the poor of England, I can't do that. Not because he is innocent of the charges—I am sure that Lord Raynes is no different from any other gentleman of his class in that respect—but because you simply can not go about judging matters in such a biblical way. It places you in the position of making moral judgements. Does this person *deserve* to be robbed? What utter rot! Who are we to judge that, and why should we? You and I are not Robin Hood. We do not steal from the rich and give to the poor. Unless, of course, you consider our own selves an appropriate charity. We are thieves. We steal for the thrill, and for the money. Once you learn to accept that aspect of your own character, it quickly banishes any drop of ambiguity."

Listening to him, Lark felt as if Damian were offering her a window with a view straight into his soul. And she could not help but experience a sense of pride, confident that he did not share such secrets with just anyone. It had to mean that Damian harbored some sort of warm feelings towards her. The notion was thrilling. But, even in her joy, Lark wondered how long the sentiments would last, once she confessed her little confusion with the rings.

To Damian's credit, he did not strike her or even curse loudly when Lark told him the whole truth.

He didn't say anything at all, as a matter of fact.

Silently, Damian took the ring Lark offered him, and held it up to the light, squinting one eye and turning it about, looking for distinguishing characteristics.

When she could bear it no longer, Lark burst out, "Well? Is it the genuine article?"

"Very hard to tell without the proper equipment. I shall have to take it back to the factory for a better look. Such is the problem with excessive competence. Even I can not recognize my own handiwork at casual glance."

Lark asked, "Where did you learn your skill with glass?

"Apprenticeship." Despite the fine, upper class accent he'd worked years in developing, Damian still uttered that particular word without the *a* so that it came out 'prenticeship. "I needed one desperately as soon as I grew too big for chimney work. The poorhouse bound and shipped me out to a mill in Lancashire. Dreadful place. I thought I'd die if I were forced to stay there till I was twenty-one, like the magistrate ordered. Ran away six times before I finally made it back to London without the overseer catching me. Apprenticed myself to a glassmaker when I was ten. Better seven years with him than waking up one morning at the workhouse to find out I'd been turned into pie filling."

Lark shivered. Her own childhood had been haunted by older children taunting the tiny mudlarks. "Best run quick, or they'll be coming and dragging you off to the workhouse. And you know what they do with the little ones there, don't you now? Why, kill them for pies, of course. Wee babes be the tenderest."

Damian noticed Lark's horrified expression and gently said, "In retrospect, I don't think that was true. About the children being made into pies. I think maybe it was only to scare us."

"Certainly scared me alright, it did."

Softly, he said, "Me, too."

Her ladylike gown, his black waistcoat, the cultured way both had learned to speak—none of it mattered. In the instant that Damian's eyes met Lark's, they were not Mr. Damian Moxley and Miss Lark Talbot, gentleman and lady, but a pair of hungry children, their teeth chattering from the cold.

At long last, the iron shields that stood guard night and day around Damian's soul completely shattered. Whereas before Lark had only managed to sneak stray glimpses of what hid inside, now she was finally seeing the entire tapestry. The pride, and the anger, and the pain. It was all there. And it was all Damian.

He made no attempt to hide it, shrugging in response to the gradual understanding that dawned upon Lark's features.

How strange then, to think that it all transpired in less than a minute. Damian barely paused following his confession of childhood fear, before he once again held up the diamond in front of him, and told Lark, "If this *is* the correct gem, I shall bring it to certain associates of mine on the black market. The general public will never know this ring is up for sale. But it should not take too long to find a discreet buyer. Preferably one outside of the country. With luck, we'll have our money in a few weeks."

The old Damian had returned. But Lark would never be able to look at his creation in the same way again.

That moment she saw the frightened boy still living inside the man had completely changed her sentiments for Damian. Or, rather, it added to them. After hearing his anguish over his encounter with Lord Shonrock, and now, this view of the workhouse child fearing for his life, Lark wanted to protect Damian, to hold and shelter him from ever experiencing that sort of agonizing pain again.

She asked, genuinely curious, "What will you do with your portion of the money, Damian?"

He smiled. "Another factory. I've been meaning to set one up in Bath for over a year. The customers there, I hear, are almost as enamored with useless brick-a-brack as is the ton in London."

"And what of Phillipa?"

"Oh," he teased. "Do the words useless brick-a-brack conjure up thoughts of her in *your* mind as well? What a coincidence."

Lark stifled her laughter. "What I meant was, she expects you to ask for her hand any day now. If only so she might have the pleasure of refusing it."

Lark was fishing for answers she probably did not want to hear. But the same perversity that drove her to commit grand larceny while living under her victims' roof, now urged Lark to gather all the details on Damian's exact plans for Phillipa.

"What do I need with Phillipa's hand, I have two of my own."

Now she knew he was deliberately ducking her question. She couldn't understand why. Surely, Damian had nothing to hide from her where Miss Phillipa was concerned.

"Lord Raynes' daughter can do far better than a common cit. Or so her doting Papa has told me on several occasions." The bitter tone she'd heard from him that morning in the kitchen returned to taint Damian's speech.

It disturbed Lark greatly.

For, if Damian truly cared not a whit for Phillipa, why should he grow so venomous when mentioning her father's distaste of him? It wasn't like him to express emotion about a subject that, logic dictated, he should actually be indifferent to.

"So you do love Phillipa then," Lark exclaimed, accepting the sinking feeling in her stomach as a just reward for her prying.

That explained everything.

Damian's sensitivity to his lack of title, his reluctance to end his relationship with the Rayneses, his refusal to enter into a loveless marriage combined with his subsequent refusal to deny the possibility of an eventual wedding between him and Phillipa.

How could Lark have been so foolish? How, in God's name, had she managed to miss the obvious? And how could she have ever, ever even entertained the prospect of a future for her and Damian?

"You are a silly little chit, aren't you?" Damian stated Lark's feelings about herself exactly.

"I am not," she flared, unsure if she were angry at him or at herself, but confident that fury was the only emotion she was currently capable of expressing without tears. "I am just as clever as you are, Damian Moxley. Mayhap I shan't leave London when I get my money. Mayhap I'll stay about here and offer you a bit of competition. How would you like that?"

"You are still planning on leaving England, then?" Damian refused to take her bait. He continued talking as if they were both in the middle of a perfectly casual discourse.

"Yes. Possibly. I don't know." She threw her hands up in the air. "There isn't very much for me here, is there?"

"No family?" he asked. "No man?"

"Goodness, no. How would I ever explain myself to one?"

"Why in the world should you?" Damian reached for Lark, raised her chin with a single finger, and peered into her eyes.

She froze, lost in his touch, as Damian turned Lark's face, studying both the right and left profile.

"Any man would be foolish to cast you away merely because of a past, shall we say, industrious nature."

"Any man?" Lark's breath caught in her throat.

"Yes." Damian dropped his hand abruptly to his side. "You are still young yet. Presentable. Don't tell me that you missed the looks you were attracting earlier this evening at the ball. Why, that boy who escorted you up to supper practically turned three shades of scarlet in your presence. Among men, that's considered a definite sign of interest."

"I hadn't noticed," Lark mumbled.

This wasn't the way she had prayed for him to answer her at all. What was wrong with Damian? If he was so good at reading that boy's thoughts and feelings, why was he acting so deliberately obtuse about Lark's?

Impulsively, Lark leapt up on her toes, straining to reach Damian's height, and, without warning or permission, plunked her hands down on his shoulders. She hoisted herself up and pressed her lips against his, willing, with every fiber of her being, for Damian to respond.

He did.

He grabbed her roughly by the arms, peeling Lark off him and flinging her backwards so that she nearly lost her balance.

If there was a shade in the rainbow darker than crimson, Lark's cheeks reached it in that moment. To throw herself so shamelessly at a man was one thing. But to have him reject her in so brutal a manner was more than she could bear. Tears flooded Lark's eyelids, and she no longer even cared if Damian noticed. Her pride ached as violently as her heart.

She waited, humiliated, for Damian to cut her down with a scathing remark. But he wasn't saying a word. To add insult to injury, he wasn't even bothering to look in Lark's direction.

Furious, she turned and followed Damian's gaze to the

spot he now fixated on, somewhere above and behind her head.

There, in the doorway to Lark's room, her carefully coiffed hair trembling with indignation, stood none other than Miss Phillipa Raynes.

16

Phillipa appeared unsure of whose ears to box first, Lark's or Damian's. So she settled for merely standing in the doorway, lips slightly parted in a furious gasp, both eyes flashing murder.

Damian raised one arm, as if to begin an explanation, then decided it would probably be pointless, and lowered it back against his side. On the surface, he appeared as unruffled as ever, the perpetual cool amusement never abandoning his features. But Lark felt certain he had to be feeling at least a little bit frightened.

As for herself, Lark felt more numb than anything else. The entire situation reminded her of a nightmare, of running as hard as she could and still ending up in the same spot, of wanting to scream and finding she couldn't. She felt as if her whole life had been leading up to this moment, to these people, and a test akin to King Arthur's sword in the stone.

Lark believed in destiny, and yet she stubbornly fought her initial instincts to surrender in the face of it. There might still be a way to wriggle out of this yet, both for her and for Damian. They only had to think of the right words, the right platitudes, the right explanations.

Damian began. Politely, he asked, "Is there something we may do for you, Phillipa?"

An odd opening gambit, to be sure, but Lark could only pray he knew what he was doing.

"You bastard," Phillipa flared, apparently making her decision on the spot over whom to attack first, and lunging at Damian, hand raised, aiming for his cheek.

He caught her wrist easily, holding it at arm's length, and out of harm's way. "That'll be enough, miss."

Lark felt certain Damian had never used such a tone with Phillipa before. This was the Damian no member of the ton knew.

Phillipa struggled to escape his grip, but Damian was no longer playing civilized party games. He squeezed hard enough to hurt, cutting the blood flow to Phillipa's wrist until it turned white and Lark winced in sympathy.

"That's enough, Damian," she shouted. "Stop. Let her go."

He did as Lark bade him, flicking Phillipa aside so that she stumbled to regain her balance. The raw fury in his eyes chilled Lark to the core. After everything he'd been through, no one would ever strike Damian Moxley again and think that they could get away with it.

Phillipa took only a moment to gather her wits, before recovering well enough to spit bitterly at both of them, "I knew there was something rotten afoot. Mama wouldn't listen, but I knew. I saw how you looked at each other that first evening." She turned to Lark, eager to attempt another blow. But wary of Damian, she settled for a verbal slap instead. "You filthy whore."

For Lark, who boasted a number of friends in that much maligned profession, the accusation was hardly inflammatory. Besides, it wasn't anything she hadn't heard before.

"I'm not certain what you mean by that, Miss Phillipa." When all else failed, feigned naivete often proved the best defense.

"I do not know why I am feeling so surprised," Phillipa struggled to calm herself. She took a step backwards, appraising Lark critically from a distance, and slowly rubbing one hand against the other, as if wiping off imaginary filth. "I should have expected no less from a woman of your dubious sort. A stray mongrel washing up on our doorstep with a tale of woe." Phillipa was recovering quite nicely from her shock now. She pivoted to face Damian. "And you. I should have listened to everyone's warnings about you."

"Perhaps that *would* have been the wisest course of action."

"A commoner. What could I have been thinking? You're no better than her. A street rat in fine clothing. How dare you come near me? You're barely fit to clean out a lady's chamber pot."

Insults to her own person, Lark managed to accept with a smile and casual shrug. But something inside her snapped the moment Phillipa turned on Damian.

"I beg to differ, Miss Phillipa." Lark's voice was calm, but drenched in steely determination. "I believe you are mistaken. It is you who isn't good enough to clean *anything* of Damian's." She chose to interpret Phillipa's shocked gasp as permission to continue. "Damian Moxley built a fortune using only his wits and his ingenuity. What useful or productive thing, exactly, have you done in your life?"

Damian interrupted, "I am more than capable of speaking for myself, Miss Talbot."

Maybe he was, but Lark was enjoying herself too much to stop now. "Damian could buy and sell half the men waltzing in your ballroom right now. They may have the fancy titles, but those can get rather hard to chew in times of famine."

"That's enough, Miss Talbot." Damian repeated his rebuke. His tone was brusque, slightly amused, and, this was the most surprising detail, ridiculously grateful.

The rest of her tirade died before crossing Larks lips.

She turned to face Damian, new understanding dawning slowly. She'd already guessed that the compliments in his past may have been few and far between. But now Lark was willing to bet money that she was the first person ever to defend Damian to anyone.

The realization shocked her briefly.

But then, Lark recalled, when exactly was the last time that anyone had ever stood up for her?

There simply wasn't any time for heroic verbalizing in the slums of St. Giles. People were too busy scavenging and struggling to survive. Previously, if Lark passed by a soul in trouble, her first instinct would be to just keep walking. If she gave the matter any thought at all, it would most likely be to curse the fool for landing inside such a stew in the first place.

And it must have been the same for Damian. Worse, probably. For, while passing strangers might, very rarely, take pity and rescue a particularly tiny and pathetic little girl, boys were expected to fend for themselves at all times. They not only didn't expect a defense, they knew enough to avoid even hoping for it.

Lark looked to Damian, seeking some sort of confirmation for her assumption, but not really needing it.

She knew she was right. Damian knew it, too.

"Thank you." His voice was soft. So soft, she might have imagined the words. But she wasn't imagining the look on Damian's face. She'd never seen it before. The harsh lines that usually framed his piercing features faded away. The brown and green forest inside his pupils bloomed springtime. "Thank you, Lark."

She didn't know how to respond. Even counting the times he'd off-handedly complimented her appearance or aptitude, Lark knew that these last three brief words were the greatest gift Damian could ever give her. Because she understood how much of his pride and honor and soul had gone into them.

And there were so many things that Lark wanted to tell Damian in response. But not now. Now wasn't the time, nor the place, and, besides, she hadn't the words. Not yet. Right now they both needed to concentrate on escaping, unscathed, from this horribly spiraling plot.

Later, Lark promised. She would tell him everything later.

Profoundly unimpressed by either Lark's heroism or Damian's gratitude, Phillipa barely paused in her rage, threatening, "I shall expose you both, don't think that I won't. Imagine, carrying on so, underneath my own roof. Have you no decency? No morals?"

Despite Phillipa's murderous ire, Lark could not help but exhale in relief. So far, she had said nothing about the diamond. Thank goodness she had not overheard enough of Lark and Damian's conversation to feel suspicious about that part of their plot. So far, Phillipa merely suspected the pair of conducting a romantic dalliance. And, to Lark's knowledge, that had yet to be deemed a hangable offense in England.

Phillipa told Lark, "You thought you could fool us with your innocent smile and shy manner. Well, once I tell everyone exactly what sort of a girl you are, there won't be a household in London willing to hire you. And word travels quickly. Don't think you'll be able to return to Bath without the scandal following you."

"She's right," Damian said in mock seriousness. "It is a proven scientific fact. Gossip travels faster than even patheons."

"And you," Phillipa whipped around to face Damian, her skirts swirling along the ground, twisting around Phillipa's legs, then spinning the other way. "I hope you enjoyed yourself this evening. Because, I assure you, it's the last ball you'll be invited to for a long, long time. My father shall see to it that you're never received in another respectable home as long as you live. And you had best surrender any plans you might have harbored of wedding a true lady. Even with all your money, only the most common sort would have you now."

Damian sighed wearily and politely asked, "Would there be an intermission scheduled in this melodrama, or is the audience expected to sit straight through without a reprieve?"

Lark racked her brain, unable to comprehend Damian's odd strategy. In his place, she would have been trying her best to appease Phillipa. To charm her into believing she had thoroughly misinterpreted the situation.

Yet oddly, Damian appeared intent on taking the opposite track. Rather than attempting to calm Miss Phillipa, he was going outside of his way to anger her more.

"You bastard," Phillipa exploded.

But only Lark understood the amused twinkle in Damian's eye when he responded, "Indeed I am."

He took a deep breath, both arms behind his back in the manner of a lecturing schoolmaster, and, hardly bothering to disguise his patronizing tone, informed Phillipa, "I can not stress enough the sheer imprudence of your choosing this moment to rush downstairs, and babble whatever it is that you think you know to be transpiring between Miss Talbot and myself."

"Of your position on that particular score, I had no doubt," Phillipa snapped.

"It is you that I am thinking of. Believe me when I say that you will look an utter fool whilst doing so." He said, "My dear, you have not been subtle in expressing your feelings for me. If you insist on accusing me of unfaithfulness with your own mother's secretary, who do you think will appear more ridiculous? Me, for snookering a fine lady like yourself whilst keeping a bit o' muslin on the side, or you, for having turned nodcock over a lowly basket scrambler such as myself?"

The validity of Damian's point succeeded in tearing an ounce of the irate wind from Phillipa's sails. She *did* have a reputation to protect. The last thing she needed was to spend the rest of the Season listening to whispers and giggles behind her back.

"Very well," Phillipa said, the wheels in her head visibly spinning as they spoke. "Perhaps this evening would not be the proper occasion for a revelation of my discovery. But I will not have your *mistress* spending another night in this house. You shall pack your things, Miss Talbot, and be gone before the next hour strikes.''

''With pleasure,'' Lark tossed her head haughtily. Now that her task was nearly done, she had hardly been looking forward to continued residence among the Raynes family.

Her practical side warned against the merits of so rashly burning her bridges whilst she still could not be one hundred percent certain of the diamond's authenticity. But the more petty side of her personality, the one residing dangerously close to her pride, refused to offer Phillipa the satisfaction of begging for permission to remain in the household for a wee bit longer.

And, as long as she was being so unceremoniously dismissed, there no longer could be anything to lose. Drawing herself up to full height, and, for the first time since their initial meeting, unleashing the full power of her fury rather than hiding behind the meek and subservient voice of an inferior, Lark flared, ''But I have a few things to say to you first, Miss Phillipa.''

''Lark . . .'' Damian warned. But she was beyond listening.

''I should like to know where it was exactly that you first concocted the notion that because you live in a four story mansion smack dab in the center of Mayfair, that it somehow grants you the permission to treat everyone who does not live similarly, like sewage floating along the gutter?''

Phillipa gasped in shock. ''Why, you wicked little chit!''

She smacked Lark across the cheek with an open palm, leaving a crimson imprint of her hand, and three bleeding slices where her fingernails had been.

Lark did not stop to think. She instinctively raised her own arm and, in popular East End vernacular, gave as good as she got.

Phillipa's eyes grew as wide as barn doors. It was clearly her first run-in with a target bold enough to return fire, and, from all indications, Miss Raynes did not at all care for this progress. Regaining her wits faster than Lark might have expected—Phillipa may have been to the manner born, but this young woman possessed the survival reflexes of a genuine street rat—Phillipa charged Lark, shoving her backwards with all of her might.

Lark stumbled, flailing her arms desperately for something to grab on to. Damian leapt forward to catch her, but failed to cross the room quickly enough, and she fell to the floor, painfully smashing her head on a table corner along the way.

Her vision blurred, yellow and black sparklers exploding in front of her eyes. The back of her skull caught fire, pain tearing through her body, and paralyzing Lark's limbs.

Instantly, Damian was hovering over her, asking Lark if she was alright. He slipped his palm beneath her neck. Was she hurt? Why didn't she answer him?

His tone, yet again, was a new and unfamiliar one. In that horrifying minute of dead silence during which Lark struggled to coerce her throbbing head into making sense of Damian's words and composing a coherent reply, she could have sworn that, in his voice, Lark heard genuine concern. And fear.

Although, for the life of her, she couldn't guess what it was that he found so frightening.

"Miss Talbot?" Phillipa's voice, not surprisingly, proved thoroughly devoid of any concern, or even remorse for her actions.

Her vision slowly clearing, Lark watched as Phillipa bent from the waist, and picked something up off the floor. But the object was too small for Lark to make out.

Phillipa, however, peered at it closely, a sly smile twitching both corners of her mouth. She turned from Damian to Lark, and asked politely, "Which one of you would like to explain what it was that this rather familiar little bauble was doing hidden within the folds of Miss Talbot's gown?"

17

Lark felt certain she was still suffering from the ill effects caused by the bump to her head. Because there could be no other reason for why she thought she was seeing the precious Raynes diamond sparkling between Miss Phillipa's fingers.

Lark blinked, hoping to clear her blurred vision. Yet the image before her refused to change.

A chill in the air froze the moment. Her senses sharpened, heightening Lark's awareness of every detail. She could hear the clock tick in ominous counterpoint to the faint strains of a polka wafting up from the ballroom, as the floor below her trembled in response to the unaccustomed number of dancing visitors.

Damian crouched beside Lark, and her skin prickled, sensitive, at the small of her back, where Damian's hand moved to support her weight and help her into a sitting position.

Her head spun, but Lark could no longer tell if it was a side effect of her fall, or in response to the sinking realization that her jig was up. There was no place to run, and certainly no place to hide. Her muddled brain could not think of a single, believable excuse for wriggling out of the situation.

And yet, oddly enough, Lark's immediate concern cen-

tered not on fretting about her own fate, but about Damian's. He would surely lose everything now. His factory,
his money, his good name. They would both be thrown
into prison—if not hung.

But for Lark, the fall from grace would prove a much
shorter journey. Damian had struggled so mightily to
reach his current, lofty position. Lark sincerely believed
he could never survive so severe a reversal of fortune.
And, from the little she'd been allowed to learn about him,
Lark felt certain that Damian would do whatever proved
necessary to prevent a return to his past life.

In the meanwhile, for the first time since they had met,
Phillipa offered Lark what seemed to be a genuine, almost
grateful, smile. "I knew I hadn't underestimated you,
Miss Talbot. I always knew your target in this house could
be nothing less than my mother's most precious possession. I must admit though, the diamond turning up underneath Mama's carpet did confuse me for a bit. Would
you believe that I even entertained a brief thought vis-à-
vis your innocence?"

Leaning on Damian's arm for support, Lark slowly rose
off the floor, ignoring the throbbing at the base of her
skull. She took a deep breath, clutching on to Damian's
shoulder for a split second longer than necessary to
merely regain her balance, and savoring the sensation of
finally having someone else to lean on—no matter how
briefly.

He helped Lark stand, hovering solicitously, refusing to
let go of her elbow until she was fully capable of standing
on her own.

"Are you quite certain you're alright?" He appeared
oblivious to the imminent threat from Phillipa, and focused exclusively on Lark. "A bump to the head can
sometimes be worse than it seems."

"I'm alright." Her voice trembled, but Lark painfully
turned to look Phillipa in the eye. "What do you want
me to say to you?"

"Well, you might start, at the very least, by offering

your congratulations. After all, I have won, haven't I?'' Phillipa's eyes and cheeks glowed with triumph. "I finally know all of your little secrets, Lark. And a few of them, I suspect, might prove most interesting to the magistrate.''

"Damn it, Phillipa," Damian's voice finally lost any pretense of civility as he cursed, "She's not a bloody mouse for you to play with before you swat for the kill. Just say your piece and get on with it. I'd like to get Miss Talbot to a surgeon to see what sort of damage you've managed to inflict.''

"Well, aren't you the gentleman, Mr. Moxley?" Phillipa tossed her head imperiously. "But I am afraid both you and your damsel in distress will be needing a great deal more than a mere surgeon by the time I have finished with you.''

The breath in Lark's throat turned cold, a frozen solid block lodging in her chest until she could neither inhale nor exhale. Her limbs felt numb, and every sound reached her ears as if through a distant haze. She had suffered through close calls before, but never anything of this magnitude. Phillipa was right. She had won, and Lark had lost—possibly her life.

Yet Damian appeared unperturbed either by her dire straits, or by his own imminent arrest. As soon as he'd ascertained that Lark was indeed well enough to stand on her own, Damian gently released his grip on her elbow, reflexively offering a curt little bow, as if thanking her for a dance. He straightened up, and withdrew his white gloves from the inside pocket of his waistcoat, slipping on first one, then the other, whilst he calmly informed Miss Phillipa, "That isn't your mother's ring. It's a very fine glass imitation. It proves nothing, save that my glassworks is contemplating a new line of merchandising— faux jewelry for those who could hardly afford the genuine article.''

Phillipa feigned disbelief, and yet her eyes narrowed as she contemplated the diamond, momentarily unsure as to whether or not Damian was telling the truth.

Lark held her breath, praying mightily for Phillipa to accept Damian's lie, while her heart beat in admiration for his quick thinking. Now Lark understood how Damian had managed to get so far in the world. Even when Lark felt ready to surrender, believing that there was simply no means of escape, he refused to say die. Lark may have had no plans to go down without a fight. But it looked as if Damian had no plans to go down, period.

Phillipa's lips pursed into a narrow line as she pondered Damian's words. But after what seemed like an eternity of waiting for her to arrive at a verdict, Miss Raynes only smiled, raising her eyes to appraise Damian and Lark, and coolly told them, "There may be an imitation diamond from the Moxley factory in this house, but I sincerely doubt that's what I am holding in my hand. Do you think I missed your little melodrama in the dining room, Miss Talbot? There have been an awful lot of accidents ever since you arrived in this house. Although, in retrospect, I doubt even one of them was truly accidental. You spilled food on Mama's gown so that she would be obligated to change her frock. And that's where you switched the diamonds."

Despite her fear and general loathing of the woman, Lark could not help but entertain a grain of admiration as well. She had been wrong in her initial assessment. Phillipa Raynes was far, far from the average young lady of the ton, whose brain appeared only large enough to harbor mindless chatter and the latest Paris fashions. No one could ever accuse her of being foolish. On the other hand, no one could ever accuse her of being pleasant, either.

"Why, Phillipa, what an overactive imagination you have." Damian refused to blink at her challenge. "If one did not know better, one might confuse you with those popular lady writers Mrs. Meeke or Mrs. Kitty Cuthbertson. Next in your plot perhaps you will reveal a lowly commoner to be the son of a duke or some sort, as it was in *Santo Sebastio*."

Lark snuck a horrified peek at Damian. Here they both

stood in mortal danger of finding themselves swinging twenty feet off the ground from a gibbet, and he was making veiled jokes referring to his own true relationship with the Earl of Shonrock.

Thankfully, Phillipa neither understood the true meaning behind his humor, nor appreciated the attempt. She sighed in disgust, as if wondering what more she could have expected from a pair of their sort, and coolly asked, "How much do you aim to profit from Mama's diamond?"

"No less than what your Papa paid for it. That's only fair." Damian emphasized the last word, and winked at Lark. She wondered how he could remain so calm. Her own legs trembled so badly she could barely stand upright.

"A heady sum," Phillipa conceded. "I declare, I could do a great deal with it."

Even Damian's otherwise cool demeanor was rattled by that last remark. "I beg your pardon?"

"Half," Phillipa explained. "I shall take half the money you earn from selling the ring—it would have been mine some day, but I do hate waiting—in exchange for keeping my lips sealed."

Lark exclaimed, "You're out of your bloody mind!"

She looked to Damian, expecting him to be as baffled as she by Phillipa's bizarre proposal. Was the woman mad? Did she think that, after everything, they would even consider striking some sort of bargain with her?

"Tell her, Damian," Lark urged. "Tell Phillipa she's out of her bloody mind."

But he was no longer looking at Lark. Damian's gaze was locked squarely upon Phillipa, the gears in his head clicking at fantastic speeds as he summed up their situation, trying to guess how likely Miss Raynes was to carry out her threats of exposure.

Damian did not even glance in Lark's direction, as he told Phillipa, "We accept your offer."

*   *   *

For the next quarter hour, Phillipa and Damian negotiated terms as if Lark weren't even in the room. She felt like a child excluded from her parents' dinner party, and only allowed to hover on the fringes, watching.

After everything was settled, Damian suggested they had best all return to the ball, lest anyone notice they were missing.

Lark tried to explain that Lady Raynes had forbidden her returning, but Phillipa waved the concerns away. "Mama often makes such threats whilst angry. She never means it for long."

"Well, we've already spent much too much time away from the festivities," Damian said.

Phillipa agreed, laughing gaily that the last thing she needed was a compromised reputation. Of any sort. Before they adjourned downstairs, she returned the ring to Lark, explaining, "If anyone is discovered with the diamond on their person, I would much prefer it to be you, rather than I."

"You are not afraid I might run off with it?" Lark asked.

"Oh, goodness, no. I intend to watch you very closely. Try to run, and you'll never make it past the door."

Restoring the gem to its hiding place in her hair ribbon, Lark followed Damian and Phillipa downstairs. She attempted to catch Damian's eye, hoping for an explanation or reassurance, but he stubbornly refused to meet her gaze.

Once back at the threshold of the ballroom, Phillipa and Damian quickly melted into the crowd and out of sight, leaving Lark to stand alone, attempting to understand what had just happened.

She had been blackmailed, that much would be clear even to a blind man. But why had Damian acquiesced so quickly?

He'd acted as if their being forced to split the money with Phillipa was the most natural thing in the world—

even if that now meant the pair of them only ending up with one fourth, rather than one half of the profit.

And he certainly was not acting the least bit concerned about it. Lark watched Damian on the dance floor with Phillipa. The minuet having just finished, he slowly promenaded her halfway across the room on his right arm. The couples reminded Lark of a funeral procession. Her own funeral procession.

Damian and Phillipa's heads bent towards one another, their lips moving in furtive whispers, and, every once in a while, one or both would turn to look at Lark, guiltily glancing away when they caught her watching them.

Paranoia was not a pretty emotion, and Lark did not enjoy feeling it in the slightest. But what else was she supposed to think? Damian was getting ready to double-cross her.

After all, why should he settle for only one-fourth of the profits, when he might cut Lark out of the equation, and resurface with half? He and Phillipa could turn on Lark, and accuse her of stealing the diamond. Lark would be jailed, and the diamond returned to Lady Raynes. But now that Damian had Phillipa on his side, it would prove no hardship to switch the rings for a second time. Then, when he finally sold it, the money would only need to be split between him and Phillipa. And, if the pair married, the entire sum would soon be his anyhow.

A pain stabbed through Lark's heart, less at the prospect of exiting this blasted job without a farthing, and more in profound disappointment that Damian should turn on her so. How silly she had been to assume that her feelings for him might ever stretch in both directions.

Across the room, Damian and Phillipa retreated to a private corner, their heads still together in intimate conversation.

After a good five minutes of Damian talking and Phillipa first shaking her head, then gradually nodding in agreement, the pair finally came up for air. Phillipa was positively beaming, her eyes sparkling with mischief and unmistakable malice.

Damian's expression proved a bit harder to read. Disinterest mingled with just a touch of apprehension and, possibly, remorse.

Unease gnawed at Lark's stomach. She stood rooted to the spot, feeling like an animal caught in a trap from which it could only wait and watch as the hunter grew closer. Her unease turned to panic as Lark's eyes followed Miss Phillipa. She crossed the room towards her mother, and politely pulled Lady Raynes aside.

Lark did not have to hear their words, to know what the two women were talking about. The utter shock on Lady Raynes' face as she looked from her ring to Phillipa and back again, told Lark everything she needed to know.

It was too late to run. Lark couldn't have done it even if she wanted to. She was trapped on all sides by swirling bodies dressed in silk and taffeta.

With Damian making up the rear, the entire Raynes family descended, en masse, upon Lark, everyone speaking at once.

"My daughter has just told me the most fantastic tale—'' Lady Raynes began, only to be interrupted by Lord Raynes, demanding to know if the accusation were true. Had Miss Talbot stolen his wife's precious diamond and switched it with a copy?

His lordship, in turn, was interrupted by Phillipa, shocked that her beloved father could even consider taking some strange girl's word over her own. If Phillipa said it was so, then, surely, it must be so. Why was Lord Raynes even bothering to question Lark? She should be arrested and searched immediately.

The only one not making a sound was Damian. He stood off to the side, hands clasped behind his back, eyes focused squarely on a spot of wall a good foot over Lark's head. If he was concerned about Lark, or feeling triumphant over his part in finally trapping her, neither emotion could be read on his face.

The Rayneses' attempts to be heard over the din of each others' raised voices, drew quite a bit of attention from their guests, and it wasn't long before a crowd gathered, listening intently.

As the assembled peers realized that Miss Phillipa was accusing Lark of having stolen Lady Raynes' ring and switching it with an imposter, they too began firing questions at Lark, until each word became like a needle jabbed into her flesh. She could not turn around without encountering an angry face.

"What have you to say for yourself, girl?" Lord Raynes raised both arms to quiet the spectators and grabbed Lark roughly by the wrist, as if afraid she might bolt. That option was hardly likely. She stood surrounded on all sides, like a drop of honey descended upon by a colony of ravenous ants. She could hardly breathe, much less move about.

In a small voice, Lark asked, "Why do you not believe that your diamond is indeed the genuine article, my lord? To be sure, it looks no different to my eyes."

This time, Lark did not need to force any tears. They came naturally of fear, as did the tremble in her lips, and the blush upon her cheeks.

"Indeed," Lady Raynes stretched her bejeweled hand forward for all to inspect. "I must confess, I can not see a difference."

"Then why do you accuse me so?" Lark all but wailed. "How can I be charged with a theft, when even your ladyship admits she can not feel certain that a crime, in fact, has been committed?"

"You have my word, Mama," Phillipa insisted. "What reason have I to concoct such an outlandish tale?"

"Oh, Phillipa, my darling, I am not suggesting that you would deliberately deceive us. That would be ludicrous, of course. But what if you are mistaken? We can hardly run off like some ninny-hammers, lobbing accusations about, before we have gathered enough adequate facts on the matter. You recall how we over-reacted on the previous occasion, and what good did that do anyone?''

"We need proof," Lord Raynes exclaimed. "I shall take the stone myself to the jeweler and—"

"No need, Papa." Miss Phillipa's voice, calmer now and quite deliberate, floated above the crowd like two crystal glasses gently clicking one against the other. "There is a simpler method for ascertaining the presence of a true diamond. Surely, everyone knows that only a genuine article is capable of cutting glass."

The crowd murmured its confirmation of her statement.

"So I propose that we try just that. Mama, the ring upon your finger, what say you attempt to scratch that mirror in the foyer with its edge. Then we shall see who among us is telling the truth. Won't we, Miss Talbot?"

18

L ark struggled to convince herself that all was not lost. It merely seemed that way.

Lady Raynes' eyes narrowed at Phillipa's suggestion to scrape her precious diamond against a mirror. The latter may not have been worth even a fraction of the beloved jewel, but it had cost them dear all the same.

And yet, how could Lady Raynes refuse the challenge? Now that the bulk of the assembled ton had already heard Phillipa's accusation, something had to be done to prevent the spread of vicious rumor. The last thing any Raynes wanted was for word to get out that their celebrated diamond was not genuine.

Her ladyship looked to his lordship for suggestion on what she should do next. There was something terribly uncouth about the act of actually striding up to the mirror, and deliberately scratching her ring against the surface. It did not seem proper, and it could certainly never, under any circumstances, be considered ladylike.

Understanding his wife's predicament, Lord Raynes held out his palm, and gestured for her to give him the gem. It was his duty as head of the family to quickly conclude this nasty business, and restore the diamond's honor as soon as possible.

Dozens of fascinated eyes watched ever so closely as

Lady Raynes carefully slid the ring off her finger and passed it to his lordship.

"The mirror, Papa, the mirror," Phillipa urged him on. She clutched Damian's arm in excitement, and beamed up at him, as if seeking approval for how well she'd played her role.

And so Lark saved her deepest feelings of disgust for Damian. There he stood, silent, confident and smug, reveling in his own cleverness. It wasn't every hunter that so skillfully managed to slaughter a half dozen birds with a single stone.

His plot, Lark was forced out of professional courtesy to admit, shone as a masterful work of art. Damian had manipulated every element so perfectly, playing Lark against Phillipa, and Phillipa against her parents, with the skill of a true virtuoso.

And now he stood ready to collect the spoils of his victory. Scratching the diamond against a mirror would quickly prove that the ring slipped from Lady Raynes' finger was a fake. Lark would be forced to turn over the genuine article. She would be sent to prison, if not drawn and quartered on the spot. Damian would no longer be obligated to share the profits with her. And, since Miss Phillipa presented even better access to her mother's diamond than Lark ever had, it would not be too very long before Damian got his hands on it again. And, this time, he would feel no qualms over splitting the profits with his partner-in-crime. As soon as he and Phillipa wed, all her fortunes became his again.

Lark ground her teeth in fury at what an idiot she'd been. She had allowed Damian to manipulate her, to make her think that Miss Phillipa meant nothing to him, because she had so desperately wanted to believe his words.

Because she had so desperately wanted to believe there might be a chance Damian could ever come to care about her.

And now look where such foolishness had gotten her! The crowd of guests surging towards the mirror carried

Lark along with them, until she was standing barely inches from Lord Raynes, her eyes fastened tightly to the diamond, as he self-consciously raised his hand in the direction of the mirror.

Phillipa and Lady Raynes stood on tiptoe, struggling to peer over his shoulder. The elder woman's face pinched with concern over how all of this looked, and what everyone would say if it turned out her gem was nothing more than highly polished glass. She prayed such was not the case.

On the other hand, the zealous expression on Phillipa's face left no doubt over which verdict she preferred.

Lark wished she could feel equally as confident when it came to knowing which side she was rooting for.

Obviously, it would prove most beneficial for her, if the ring was revealed to be genuine. There would be no theft for the Rayneses to accuse her of then. They'd look the fools and be forced to apologize. Again. Perhaps, if she played her cards right, Lark might even prove capable of playing on their guilt and exiting this horrid jumble with a bit of monetary reward for her trouble.

But, then again, if Lark was unmasked as a thief, it would offer her the opportunity to incriminate Damian as well. Somehow, the prospect of going to prison did not seem nearly as dim, as long as Damian was brought down with her. At the very least, it would remove him from Phillipa's clutches once and for all.

Lark winced. She knew that her thoughts were petty, not to mention violently self-destructive. And yet she could not help the twinges that bubbled inside her all the same. Good Lord, but Damian Moxley had bewitched her. She might have hated it, if the feelings weren't also simultaneously so pleasant.

Lord Raynes cleared his throat, glancing from side to side and feeling like a fool, then pressed his diamond against the mirror.

Every soul in the room held their breath, and Lark among them. She recalled that fraught moment when she'd gotten confused over which ring was which, and been forced to make an on-the-spot decision. Had she picked the correct one?

The stone made a most horrid scrape as it met the glass. A few of the more delicate ladies in the room pressed both hands against their ears, and even some of the gentlemen instinctively turned away from the noise. Lady Raynes clutched one hand to her chest. Only Miss Phillipa remained as she was, eagerly watching the process before her, as she once might have cheered boat races along the Thames.

Lark snuck a glance at Damian, noting the pained expression dominating his features. Lark knew it couldn't be from the noise. In his line of work, the sound must have been second nature. She tried to guess at the cause behind his visible discomfort, but could think of not a single one.

It reminded her, rather disturbingly, of the way he'd seemed that afternoon at the jail. Bone weary and remorseful. Lark had felt unable to discern the cause of that mood either.

For the first time since they'd returned from her room, Damian turned his head so that he might meet Lark's gaze.

With all of her strength, she fought to burrow through the infuriating neutrality of his eyes, attempting to reach the ever so warm and possibly human layers Lark had caught glimpses of before. She prayed for him to let her in, to prove her previous negative thoughts about him wrong.

Damian was not helping.

Despite her best efforts, not a glimmer remained of the man she'd been privileged to make acquaintance with only an hour earlier. This gentleman offered no clue of their even having met before. To all surface appearances, he was merely another ball guest standing about, scandalously curious.

Despite a lack of an arranged signal, everybody in the

room shifted ever so slightly forward, peering at the mirror, searching for any sign of scratched surface beneath the diamond.

Light bouncing and refracting off the chandeliers and mirror made it temporarily impossible to see a thing, and necks craned to avoid the glare, hands bobbing up to shield eyes.

Lark herself squinted, cocking her chin to one side in an attempt to see beneath the glare. The blood racing through her veins pumped at an unprecedented pace, until Lark feared her head popping off from the pressure.

Finally, his lordship exhaled mightily, pulling his arm back from the mirror and revealing the glass surface for all to see.

Where once had shone smooth silver, now gaped a jagged, inch-long streak flecked with white powder along both sides.

Lark clamped her lips shut to prevent a disappointed groan from sneaking past. After everything, all the hard work, all the intrigue and tension and sleepless night worry, she had snatched the wrong diamond after all.

No wonder Damian mocked her so. She deserved it for being such a skittle-witted ninny. Lark hung her head, at long last overcome with guilt—not for attempting the theft, but for bungling it so badly.

Miss Phillipa groaned as well, obviously for wildly different reasons. She looked from the disfigured mirror to Lark and back again, then pivoted her head to glare accusingly at Damian.

At least he had the decency to also meet her glance with his neutral stare.

"Goodness me," Lady Raynes fretted, raising her anxious hand from throat to cheek. She too swiveled her eyes from ruined mirror to diamond ring. But her accusatory glare was saved for Phillipa.

"I don't understand it, Mama," Phillipa stammered. "I felt certain— I saw it— Miss Talbot—"

"I think there have been quite enough charges leveled

against Miss Talbot this evening.'' Lord Raynes looked the way Lark felt. As if he wished more than anything to just close his eyes and wake up to find the entire fiasco cleared up.

"No." Phillipa angrily stamped her foot, pleadingly sweeping the assembled crowd with her eyes for moral assistance. The front row, unsure of what the proper reaction might be, responded by awkwardly staring down at the floor or up at the ceiling.

"I assure you, Papa, Mama," Phillipa whined, "Miss Talbot is plotting to steal our diamond from us."

She needed to raise her voice in order to be heard above the weary guests. They were swiftly growing bored of this drama without a denouement, drifting back towards the ballroom, and whispering among themselves behind closely cupped palms.

"Her hair ribbon," Phillipa announced, basking in a triumphant second wind. "I demand that she show you what's inside her hair ribbon. Then you shall all see."

The color drained from Lark's cheeks and, for the first time ever, she genuinely felt as if she might faint at any moment.

She tried shaking her head from side to side, protesting, "No. No, it isn't seemly. I can't."

"Oh, come now," Phillipa snapped. "It isn't as if you were being asked to strip to your stays."

A shocked gasp rose from the crowd of guests in response to her language. Lady Raynes frantically fanned herself, Lord Raynes grew red-faced, deeply embarrassed by his daughter's behavior, and sneaking furtive glances from side to side, gauging everyone's reaction.

But Phillipa was on a rampage. It was the principle now, instead of merely financial interest or obscure spite. Phillipa was determined to bring Lark down, one way or the other, and she no longer even cared if her reputation was smashed in the process.

"The ribbon," she insisted in a voice frigid enough to

send chills up and down Lark's spine, and held out her hand.

Despite knowing that no aid would be forthcoming, Lark could not help herself looking pleadingly into the crowd, all but begging for someone, anyone, to speak up and save her.

But no one dared. They were too frightened of Phillipa.

Lark raised both arms reluctantly above her head, silently fumbling with the ribbon, and needing to dig her fingernails into the knots, yanking them free. She could feel the false diamond underneath the material, and knew there was no chance of Phillipa failing to find it. She had seen Lark slip it into place.

Slowly, she tugged the ribbon free.

"Give it here," Phillipa ordered, and Lark had no choice but to hand over the hair ribbon, fingers trembling.

Miss Raynes snatched her treasure triumphantly, tearing along the seam, and jabbing her grip into the opening, hungrily feeling around the bottom like a woman possessed.

"Darling, my darling, please," Lady Raynes clucked, but the gentle rebuke came too late to do any good. She looked helplessly at Lord Raynes, who only twisted his face into a pained grimace, and shook his head from side to side.

Damian had yet to say a word, yet Lark felt his presence most keenly of all.

Help me, Damian, Lark silently prayed. *Please, help me.*

She harbored not a single doubt that he was capable of it. The unanswered question stood, was he willing?

"Aha!" Phillipa's victorious cry stabbed through Lark's skull with the force and agony of impalement upon a spiked iron gate.

Looking both ways at the guests to insure everyone's undivided attention, Phillipa drew her fingers out from inside the ribbon, thrusting the false diamond forward in replica of the proverbial head on a silver platter.

"What in blazes is this?" Lord Raynes strode forward, comparing the diamond in Phillipa's hand with the one he still clutched in his own.

"You see, Papa? You see? I was correct. She *is* plotting to steal Mama's ring. Here is all the evidence we shall ever need!"

19

"Just what is the meaning of this?" Lord Raynes bellowed with an almost physical force, prompting Lark to take a step backwards.

The artificial diamond between them seemed to grow in physical dimension, until it was no longer merely the size of an egg, but that of a chicken. It assumed a life of its own. Every reflected glimmer of light was a piercing accusation straight through to her heart.

She struggled to defend herself. Her lips moved, and yet no sound came out. What was there to say? The pair of identical diamonds told it all.

"Pardon me, my lord." Damian's voice wafted lazily from the rear of the room, his tone casual, as if he were merely asking permission to pass through the crowd.

He rested one gloved hand upon the back of the well-coiffed lady in front of him, and gently moved her aside. The remainder of the guests obediently scampered in either direction, forming a clear passage leading to Lord Raynes.

Damian strolled the distance between them at an unhurried pace. Lark, remembering a single, brief bible-lesson from a wandering preacher attempting to save the mudlarks' souls, could not help but think of Moses parting the Red Sea.

She was surprised to observe just how much Damian towered over Lord Raynes. Odd, that she'd seen them standing side by side dozens of times, and yet never noticed it before. It were almost as if Damian had deliberately made himself appear smaller whilst in his lordship's presence, hiding the strength of his true powers like a warlock in a children's fairy tale.

His voice also was louder and more authoritative than Lark had previously ever heard it. He held out one hand and informed Lord Raynes, "I believe that you, sir, are in possession of an item that rightfully belongs to me."

He snapped his fingers and pointed to the ring, thrusting his hand, palm up, further forward.

From behind her father, Phillipa gasped.

Then it was Lord Raynes' turn to sputter. "I beg your pardon?"

Damian plucked the false diamond from his lordship's grasp, holding it up in the air so that the crowd might field a better look. "Excellent workmanship, wouldn't you say? Even I could get in a spot of trouble trying to tell it from the genuine article." Damian nodded in hearty agreement with himself. "Quality. That's what every customer patronizing my humble little establishment is promised, and that's what every customer will receive, by God."

"Have you taken a knock in the cradle, man?" Lord Raynes demanded. "Are you telling me that this article of deception is a handiwork of yours, sir?"

"Indeed," Damian answered in all earnestness. "For while I do confess that I have often allowed my underlings carte-blanche in the construction of less complicated items—simple lamps, smaller mirrors, candlesticks, that sort of thing—when time comes to create a truly inspired work, I trust no one less than myself with the details. There are some things that a man simply *must* tackle on his own, if he wishes them done correctly."

"But what is the meaning of this?" Phillipa exclaimed. And, again, Lark suspected that there was more than one question trapped within her simple query. Yes, Phillipa wished to know why Damian was rambling on about fine craftsmanship in the field of glasswork, but she was also dying to learn why he had chosen to stray so far from their previously agreed upon plan of action.

"The meaning, Miss Phillipa? Why, nothing, save that I would very much like my property returned. We have already proven beyond a shadow of a doubt"—he indicated the scratched inch of mirror—"that no theft has taken place upon this night."

"*That*, sir, was because I prevented it from happening. Can you not see?" She appeared to be speaking to Damian, but was truly addressing everyone in the foyer. She grabbed the ring out of his hands, waving it about madly. "Miss Talbot came here scheming to substitute this false diamond for my mother's genuine jewel."

Damian's face stretched into a smile so wide it could only be patronizing. "No, my dear, I'm afraid that you are mistaken."

"Damian Moxley!" Phillipa's surface demeanor remained barely flustered, yet her voice called to mind a petulant child. "Then mayhap you would wish to offer an alternate explanation for the existence of this duplicate, albeit worthless, bauble."

"Actually, Miss Phillipa, I would rather not, if it is all the same to you. I am afraid that an honest explanation might prove rather embarrassing to all concerned."

An honest explanation. With all the confusion of the last hour, Lark could truly no longer recall what an honest explanation might be. Her head spun madly, preconceived notions wrestling for contemplation time with muddled theories, erroneous assumptions, and dare-she-even-think-it dreams. She harbored not a clue as to what Damian thought he was doing, and why?

Lark struggled to guess where Damian's loyalties might lie, but only managed to confirm a single fact. More than anything else, Damian stood prepared to defend his own, exclusive interests.

"I demand that you stop this speaking in riddles, Mr. Moxley. You have already confessed to creating the glass diamond in your own factory. I believe my parents and I deserve an explanation as to your reasons."

Lark wondered what Damian could possibly say now that might absolve him of suspicion and prevent the Rayneses' accusation that he was plotting with Lark.

The calm that had settled over Lark when Damian first stepped forward in her defense now abandoned her. A chill enveloped her, and she began to tremble uncontrollably. She folded her arms and rubbed both shoulders with her hands, teeth chattering. But this time, the numbing fear was no longer for her own fate. It was for Damian's.

"Let him be!" The anguished plea escaped Lark's mouth despite her lack of recollection in planning to utter it. "Mr. Moxley is not at fault. He is merely playing the gentleman for my sake."

Phillipa pivoted to face Lark. "Are you finally ready to confess the truth, Miss Talbot?"

"Yes." Lark's gaze met Damian's, and, despite the nearly imperceptible twitch of his head, urging her to keep quiet, she stubbornly proceeded. "I approached Mr. Moxley, requesting that he create an imitation ring for me. I told him I wished to have a bit of fun with my friends, fool them into thinking I had snatched the Raynes diamond. He knew nothing of my true intentions."

"That's enough, Lark," Damian said softly. "I thank you for your spirited defense from the bottom of my heart." Damian spoke louder. "Forgive me, Miss Talbot, but I have grown rather tired of the lies. What say you, we make a clean confession and put an end to this dreary melodrama once and for all?"

"A confession?" She repeated dumbly. A confession of what? Which version of which tale was Damian proposing they confess?

"Indeed it is true that I constructed the imitation diamond. And indeed it is also true that I did it for Lark. Albeit not at her beckoning, and certainly not for reasons of larceny. Rather, she had often spoken of how beautiful and stylish she found Lady Raynes' ring. So, when it came time for me to present her with a token of engagement, I simply copied the stone and setting.''

In response to Damian's stunning announcement, Lark's gasp of surprise proved by far the loudest in the room.

However, Miss Phillipa did run a very close second. ''What are you saying, Damian?''

''I am saying that I have asked Miss Lark Talbot to be my wife. Now, I am merely waiting for her answer.'' Damian turned to Lark, cupping one of her hands between both of his, gently stroking her palm with his fingers. ''I had not planned on there being so many witnesses to this joyous occasion, but, nevertheless, I am in agony waiting for your response. Will you marry me, my dear?''

It was official. Lark had gone so far out of her head, she could no longer even discern reality from fantasy. If she did not know better, she might have sworn that Damian had just asked her, in front of the entire ton, to marry him.

Yet, if this were a dream, it was a particularly realistic one. She could hear the rustling of multi-layered gowns all around her, smell the sweet aroma of tea, lemonade, and cakes from the refreshment room, feel the warmth from Damian's hands course through her body, urging her mouth to bring forth a reply her mind still could not grasp.

She could not think. And so she gave in to her instincts and, without any idea of what she was doing, murmured, ''I—yes. Yes, Damian, of course.''

''Splendid.'' Damian beamed at the stupefied crowd, as if the impromptu proposal were the most natural occurrence in the world.

He plucked the second diamond from Miss Phillipa's grasp, and easily slipped it upon Lark's finger.

She gazed down upon it, unsure of what to say or do next.

Fortunately, Phillipa suffered from no such malady.

Cheeks turning a shade of crimson previously seen only among Far East curtains and rugs, she smashed both palms against Damian's back, shoving him towards the front door and screaming, "Get out! You, you . . . horrid bastard."

He turned around slowly, amused at the outburst. Both Lord and Lady Raynes leapt to restrain her, maneuvering the furious Phillipa into a private room and away from prying eyes. Lark grabbed Damian by the sleeve, suggesting that now might be a good time for them to take their leave. But Damian shook his head, pulling Lark with him into the room harboring Lord, Lady, and Miss Phillipa Raynes, and closing the door behind them.

At the sight of Damian, Phillipa flailed like a madwoman, aiming her blows where they might do the most damage.

Damian stood in front of Lark, shielding her from Phillipa's attack, and momentarily accepting a few of the blows against his chest before grabbing both of Phillipa's wrists in the grip of one hand and yanking them upwards out of harm's way. He hefted Miss Phillipa's arms over her head, until only the tips of her feet touched the floor, and she dangled precariously off balance.

"If I am to let you go," Damian asked politely, "will you promise to behave?"

In lieu of a reply, Miss Phillipa Raynes, daughter of a peer and one of the ton's grandest ladies, spit in Damian's face.

He smiled, almost as if the outburst had been a long expected gift, and gently released Phillipa's wrists. Reaching into his pocket, Damian withdrew a monogrammed handkerchief, and silently dabbed at his face, wiping it clean. He then refolded the cloth, and tucked it back inside his jacket.

Lark watched, in awe, both of his self-control and of his finely tuned sense of the dramatic.

With exaggerated formality, Damian bowed in Miss Phillipa's direction, then turned and did the same in front of Lord Raynes, Lady Raynes. "As always, it has been a splendid ball, my lord. You have truly outdone yourself."

Damian turned to Lark, offering her his arm as if asking to escort her to dinner. She slipped her hand silently into the crook of his elbow, comforted by how natural it felt.

"We'll see ourselves out," Damian assured Lady Raynes. "Do pass on our goodnights to all."

He opened the door and together they stepped back into the brightly lit hall, where crowds of the curious still gathered. Lark was uncomfortably aware of the multiple eyes watching them leave. Funny how Lark had made the trip from foyer to front door some dozens of times previous, yet it had never felt this bloody long before. And with each step she took, Lark saw her future fading away into nothingness. After this spectacle, was there a spot left in England where she could work unnoticed?

Damian raised his right arm, waving the onlookers all back into the ballroom. "Carry on, then. You've certainly got my permission."

The door slammed loudly shut behind them, shoving Lark and Damian onto the front steps. They looked at each other, lips pursed in contemplation, mulling what had just happened. Then, unable to restrain themselves any longer, both burst out laughing.

Lark waited at the curb for Damian to fetch his carriage and horses from the grooms. Every few seconds, a particularly vivid memory of Phillipa's comic fury surfaced in Lark's mind, and she found herself awash in a fresh flood of giggles.

Truly, it was the laughter of the mad, if not the damned.

Here Lark stood, a meaningless glass rock on her finger, not a farthing in her pocket, and very little chance now of ever earning one. She had no place to go and no one to turn to. And yet, Lark could not recall ever feeling this happy.

Was it Damian who made her feel this way? If it was, then Lark was a sillier widgeon than even she had previously assumed. For, despite everything they had been through, Lark still harbored not a sliver of notion about how he truly felt towards her.

Even a fool could see that his earlier proposal was nothing but a bit of play-acting. He did it to save Lark's neck—as well as his own. And yet, as she spied his coach rounding the corner, Lark could not stop the anxious stirring in her stomach from hoping that maybe, just maybe, it had been something more.

20

Damian took Lark by the hand and helped her climb inside the carriage, all the while waving gaily to the few faces still pressed against the window inside the Raynes' house, watching them leave.

His coachman asked, "Where to, sir?"

And Damian said, "Home."

Lark jumped at the word. "Your home?"

"Am I mistaken in assuming that, among us, I'm the only soul that still has one? After all," Damian indicated Lark's tiny bedroom on the Raynes' top floor, "your home is certainly no longer a viable option."

Lark hesitated, biting her lower lip, and glancing nervously about the carriage. "I—yes. You are correct about that. But. Damian. Do you think it would be . . . proper?"

He raised both eyebrows, trying not to laugh out loud at Lark's unexpected earnestness. "Proper? You are worried about how it will look? After the show we just put on this evening?"

"This isn't the same as when I came to see you at the factory. The pair of us arriving, unchaperoned, at your home, could prove terribly compromising."

"For whom?" Damian asked, "Me, or you?"

"Well, you, of course. I haven't a reputation to speak of."

"Oh, no, my dear. On that, I'm afraid I must differ. After tonight, you possess a reputation of royal proportions." He leaned back comfortably in the carriage, head bobbing slightly against the cushions, in rhythm to the jostling wheels. "As for me, it would be foolish to think that I shall soon be regaining my favored spot among the ton. Maybe in time. But not for a bit yet."

Guiltily, Lark asked, "Will you miss it, then?"

"Oh, yes," Damian's voice simmered sarcasm. "One can not even begin to describe the pleasures of playing lap-dog for the rich and titled. Half the time, I sat about expecting to be asked to fetch the master's slippers."

His gaiety surprised Lark. She'd fully expected Damian to be furious, both at the evening's failed outcome, and at her for causing it. But he appeared in genuine good spirits, and certainly more relaxed than Lark had previously ever seen him. Almost as if a great weight had been lifted off his shoulders.

Instead of sulking, Damian was actually smiling. He looked Lark in the eye when he spoke to her; his gestures were more animated, freer, as he emphasized points with his hands. This personality swing rather unsettled Lark. It wasn't that she disliked this new Damian. If anything, she liked him more than any previously revealed incarnation.

And that was the crux of the problem.

With every passing moment, Lark fell more and more in love with Damian Moxley. And yet, despite his bizarre behavior earlier in the evening, Lark still could not understand exactly how he felt about *her*.

He'd rushed to Lark's defense, that much was true. But he would have surely done the same for any business partner. There might have been nothing personal in his heroism. For all Lark knew, he was simply repaying a debt. She'd stood up for him, and now Damian was standing up for her.

Considering the mass of contradictions that was Damian, Lark would not be surprised if she learned that his true motive was simply a reluctance to feel beholden in front of Lark. Certainly, when it came to leaping to each other's defense, Lark and Damian were now running dead even.

She only wished that she could say the same about their feelings towards each other.

The windows of Damian's modest two-story home looked out upon Belgrave Square, the most southern residential district in London that could still be considered a part of the West End. A kitchen occupied the whole of the basement, with a dining and drawing room on the ground level.

A maid opened the door to them, taking Damian's hat and coat, then quietly disappearing. Her lack of reaction to the sight of Damian arriving alone with a strange young woman made Lark wonder what sort of company he usually kept, whilst away from the aristocracy's prying eyes.

She wasn't sure what she'd expected Damian's residence to look like, yet Lark was nevertheless surprised by the simplicity and sheer tastefulness of the surroundings. So many aspirants to the aristocracy tended to flaunt their wealth by cramming every room with expensive nonsense ranging from china figurines, malacca walking sticks, stuffed animal remnants of the latest hunt, and enough candlesticks to light a surgeon's operating room.

Yet, Damian, who certainly did not hide his social-climbing ambitions, had chosen to decorate his home sparsely, for comfort. The paintings hanging on his walls were mounted not in ostentatious wreaths of gold and sliver, but rather in frames that complimented the artwork. His muted burgundy carpet matched the window-drapes in shade exactly. One entire wall was dominated by a bookshelf filled to the overflowing. Lark noticed the tomes were not grouped by cover color, but alphabetically by author.

Damian escorted Lark into the drawing room, and rang for a second housemaid to come light them a fire. Its warmth pulled Lark to stand in front of it, stretching her hands forward and basking in the comforting heat. They'd left the Rayneses' in such a hurry, there'd been no time for her to grab a wrap, and the night air during the carriage ride over had chilled Lark to the bone.

She shivered, rubbing her palms one against the other.

Damian, looking up from where he stood pouring sherry into a pair of exquisitely carved crystal glasses, stopped what he was doing and moved to stand beside her.

"Are you cold?" he asked.

"Just a bit." Lark could not understand where this unexpected shyness had descended from, but she could hear the slight tremor in her voice, and feel her hands shaking, not only from the cold.

"This house can be terribly drafty. I suppose that I should keep it heated at all times, but I am home so rarely, it seems like a terrible waste of coal and money."

Damian reached for Lark's hands, maneuvering them away from the fire and in between his two palms. He rubbed her fingers against his, spreading the warmth from his skin to hers. His grasp barely reached to her wrists, and yet Lark could feel his tender touch along every inch of her. It made her gasp with pleasure, and dig her heels into the rug to keep from swooning.

The Lark watching from the side could see that she was making an absolute ninny of herself. Yet the Lark standing next to the fire prayed that this feeling might go on forever.

Damian loosened his grip, and brought Lark's right palm to eye level, studying the faux-diamond ring on her finger at close range. The sight made him chuckle, and he patted her hand before gently returning Lark's arm to her side.

Their break in physical contact flooded Lark with an unnamed, wordless regret, and she had to clamp both lips tightly shut to keep from begging him to continue.

Damian clenched his own hands in mock prayer, using the pair of upright thumbs to lightly tap against his chin, and asked Lark, "Well, then, what shall we do about our mutual dilemma?"

"I beg your pardon?" Lark could think of more than a few dilemmas in her own immediate future—a lack of home, prospects, and income loomed right at the top of the list—but she saw nothing that included Damian.

"We made quite a spectacle of ourselves this evening." His eyes twinkled in fond memory.

"Indeed we did. Although," Lark hesitated, "I must ask. Why did you do it, Damian?"

He seemed surprised, and a little offended by her question. "Would you prefer that I had stood by and allowed you to be taken off to jail?"

"You *had* attempted to send me there yourself on a number of occasions," she reminded.

"Ah, yes, well. That was different. That was pure business."

"And tonight was not business?" Lark held her breath, waiting for Damian's reply.

"Certainly not. Tonight was a fiasco."

She winced. There. Now Damian would finally get around to berating her foolishness. Lark braced herself for the onslaught.

Yet, instead of blasting her, Damian merely shrugged his shoulders and took a sip of sherry. He'd rested his glass on the fireplace mantle, and now stood with one elbow leaning against it.

"I must admit, the marriage proposal cover-up did prove a bit of quick thinking genius on my part."

"Yes." Lark swallowed hard. "It was terribly clever of you."

"But it does create a problem. Now that we have made such a public announcement of marriage, it would look terribly odd if we, in the end, decided not go through with it."

Lark blinked, her ears ringing. Was she mistaken, or had she just received her second marriage proposal?

"I'm sorry." Lark cocked her head to one side. "What did you just say, Damian?"

"I said that it would look frightfully odd for us, if, after everything, you and I did not get married. It might raise some nasty suspicions that all is not on the up-and-up."

"You think that we should get married?"

"It is the only way to keep our assorted ton friends from wondering about things they have no need to wonder about."

"I see." Lark did not see at all, but it seemed like the right thing to say. Damian was asking her to marry him. Again. A few hours ago, she might have leapt for joy at the development. But now, she could only shake her head in confusion.

He said, "I have no doubt that you and I will be watched very closely in the coming weeks. All of London will be talking about us. I daresay, we might even prove the topic of the Season."

"Yes, and I suspect they'll be using words that, on most other occasions, they unanimously claim not to know."

"Indeed," Damian laughed.

Lark wished she could feel as happy as Damian seemed to.

Yet, something still did not seem quite right. There was a piece missing to this very unconventional proposal. And Lark was determined to pry it out of Damian before offering him a concrete answer one way or the other.

Hesitantly, she asked Damian, "So you would like us to marry for convenience?"

"Yes."

"But did you, Damian, did you not once tell me, that you would never, no matter what the reasons, enter into a loveless marriage?"

"I said that. And I meant it." He raised his chin defiantly. "I mean it still."

It took Lark a beat to understand what Damian was

trying to tell her. But, when the words he could not say finally blossomed clear in Lark's mind, her eyes grew wide, and she could only stare at Damian, temporarily uncharacteristically mute.

He cupped her face between his hands, kissing Lark fully and deeply, his lips speaking more with a kiss than they ever would with words. They told her everything Lark would ever need to know about Damian. About this man whose actions were so much more important than his words.

When they broke apart, Lark's mouth felt bruised and swollen, and yet she hungered to feel Damian's pressed against hers one more time. They stood, faces only inches apart. Damian's hands gently stroked the back of her neck, under her hair, with his fingers, and her cheeks with his thumbs.

Softly, he prompted, "Say yes, Lark."

"Yes." She'd never received such sensual pleasure from uttering a simple sound before. "Yes. Yes, Damian. Yes."

He rested his forehead against hers, their noses almost touching, and whispered, "Good."

She could only imagine what a comical picture they presented, leaning one against the other like a pair of tent poles, Damian needing to hunch his shoulders to remain at eye-level with Lark. And yet, she felt content to remain standing in such a silly pose, breathing the same air, forever.

She sighed regretfully, and Damian chuckled.

"Disappointed with me already? It usually takes a bit longer time than that."

"Oh, no, no. I could never be disappointed with you."

"Then why, pray tell?" Damian pulled back from her to stand at arms length, his hands resting on Lark's shoulders, playfully rolling a lock of her hair around two fingers.

"I was just thinking how everything is almost perfect."

"Almost? Should I be taking offense?"

She laughed and turned her head to kiss the palm of Damian's right hand, rubbing her cheek against it. "It is regrettable that neither of us shall ever again have access to the Raynes diamond."

"Well, yes, I do find it difficult to imagine a circumstance under which we might be welcome back into their home."

"A public flogging, possibly?"

"True. With Phillipa holding the lash." Damian reached for Lark's bejeweled hand and held it up to the light so that both might enjoy his handiwork. "However, I fail to understand why we should need access to the ring upon Lady Raynes' finger, when we already have the genuine diamond right here."

"Damian," Lark said evenly, "You are confused."

"Am I?" He folded both arms across his chest. "No. No, I don't think so. Let me see. After we returned to the ballroom, I convinced Phillipa to tell her mother about the diamond switch—"

"You? You started it all?"

"Hush, Lark. This is your listening time, not your talking time. I convinced Phillipa to tell her mama about the alleged diamond switch, so that she would be forced to publicly test the genuine quality of the ring upon her finger. If I've told you once, I've told you a dozen times, the diamond is only worth money to us if no one knows it's missing. I could not risk a suspicion of theft hanging over our heads. It drives the gem prices much too far downward. This way, we are guaranteed a high profit."

"So you *wanted* Lady Raynes to publicly test her diamond?"

"Of course, I did. Now, both she and Lord Raynes are terribly happy in the knowledge that they still possess genuine treasure, and they'll never listen to another word Phillipa says about us."

Lark pressed both palms to her face, shaking her head from side to side in confusion. "But wait just one minute. I still don't understand. How can you be so sure that you and I ended up with the true diamond? After all, Lady Raynes' ring cut glass."

Damian pointed to the stone upon Lark's hand, sliding it up and down her finger, and twisting it this way and that before mischievously confessing, "Fortunately for us, there is a true bit of fact that has yet to surface strongly enough in the public to correct a rather romantic, albeit completely erroneous assumption. It is true that diamonds cut glass. However, it is equally true that, a majority of the time, glass, my dear, will also cut glass."

EPILOGUE

In the Autumn of 1825, Damian and Lark threw a large dinner party to celebrate their ascension to the rank of Sir Damian and Lady Moxley.

The newly titled couple circulated among their guests, accepting congratulations from freshly minted baronets, as well as from viscounts with patents going back over a century.

Among the hundred or so visitors passing through the Moxleys' new Mayfair home, were a handful of lords and ladies who'd also been present in the Raynes' household seven years earlier. Most were gentlemen of very old peerage and very little money. Their business with Damian was the only thing keeping them living in the grand style appropriate to their ancient titles.

Sir Damian and Lady Moxley officially opened the festivities by dancing the first waltz of the evening, then laughingly beckoned for the rest of their guests to join them.

As Damian twirled Lark about the floor, he asked her, "That strawberry coronet his grace was wearing this afternoon for the dubbing, how much do you think it might fetch on the open market?"

"I'm sure that I don't know." Lark smiled, guilelessly. "I was too busy beaming with pride as my husband received the colee of knighthood to engage in anything as crass as surreptitiously appraising the jewels atop the attending peers' heads.''

"How much, Lark?"

"A quarter of a million pounds, give or take a farthing."

Damian laughed, burying his face in his wife's hair and whispering, "You truly are an amazing creature."

"Well, the ceremony did drag on and on. I had to think of something to keep myself amused."

"Then it was not you I heard struggling to suppress laughter, whilst the sword was being tapped along my shoulders?"

"My love, I simply could not help it. My mind kept drifting back towards the tales of King Arthur and his original Knights of the Round Table. I tried to imagine you among them, taking the oath of chivalry, pledging to obey the Sacraments and the Ten Commandments. I must say, it did prove rather comical in context."

"I shall have you know that I am a staunch follower of the Ten Commandments. Never have I coveted my neighbor's wife. Why should I, when all the rest of them covet mine?"

Lark squeezed Damian's hand, reminding, "And what of 'thou shalt not steal'?"

"I have never stolen my neighbor's wife, either."

Damian slipped his arm tighter about Lark's waist and led her off the dance floor. They paused at the outskirts, watching the other couples. Lark mused, "We are ever so respectable now."

"Indeed. I looked in the mirror this morning, and I felt honored to be in the same room with me."

She sighed. "So is this it then, Damian? Are we finished? Have we sunk so low as to drown in a morass of propriety?"

"I suppose knighthood does imply a certain code of honor." He reached for a glass of wine. "That bit about chivalry and all."

''What in the world shall we do with all of our free time?''

Damian shrugged. He finished his wine, holding the goblet at arm's length, and viewing their assembled guests through the distorted spectrum of finely chiseled crystal. ''A quarter of a million pounds, did you say?''

''Give or take a farthing.''

''Naturally.''

They exchanged sly looks, each one instinctively knowing what the other was thinking. Lark's heart began to beat quicker. She felt the familiar hum starting in her bones.

''Oh, Damian, I do love you so.''

She jumped up and flung both arms about his neck, unconcerned with how odd it might look. Damian returned her embrace, his cheek rubbing softly against hers. He kissed Lark below the ear, then turned his head slightly to find her mouth. By the time Damian set her down, both were flushed and laughing.

''Excuse me, Sir Damian.'' The gentleman whose coronet initially prompted their exuberance came up to the Moxleys, clearing his throat and looking a bit sheepish. ''I had crossed the room with the expressed intention of asking your lovely wife to favor me with a dance. However, I do not wish to, um, interrupt.''

''Nonsense, your grace.'' Lark's eyes lit up and she happily took the gentleman's hand when he offered it. ''I shall be honored to dance with you.''

The older man told Damian, ''She is a treasure, your wife.''

''A treasure, indeed.'' Damian's eyes met Lark's, sharing a joke only the two of them understood. ''I daresay, she possesses the exquisite capacity to turn all men into thieves at heart.''

Avon Romances—
the best in exceptional authors and unforgettable novels!

Avon Romantic Treasures

*Unforgettable, enthralling love stories,
sparkling with passion and adventure
from Romance's bestselling authors*

LADY OF SUMMER *by Emma Merritt*
77984-6/$5.50 US/$7.50 Can

TIMESWEPT BRIDE *by Eugenia Riley*
77157-8/$5.50 US/$7.50 Can

A KISS IN THE NIGHT *by Jennifer Horsman*
77597-2/$5.50 US/$7.50 Can

SHAWNEE MOON *by Judith E. French*
77705-3/$5.50 US/$7.50 Can

PROMISE ME *by Kathleen Harrington*
77833-5/ $5.50 US/ $7.50 Can

COMANCHE RAIN *by Genell Dellin*
77525-5/ $4.99 US/ $5.99 Can

MY LORD CONQUEROR *by Samantha James*
77548-4/ $4.99 US/ $5.99 Can

ONCE UPON A KISS *by Tanya Anne Crosby*
77680-4/$4.99 US/$5.99 Can

The Sizzling Night Trilogy by
New York Times Bestselling Author

NIGHT STORM
75623-4/$5.99 US/$7.99 Can

Fiery, free-spirited Eugenia Paxton put her heart to the sea in the hands of a captain she dared not trust. But once on the tempestuous waters, the aristocratic rogue Alec Carrick inflamed her with desires she'd never known before.

NIGHT SHADOW
75621-8/$5.99 US/$7.99 Can

The brutal murder of her benefactor left Lily Tremaine penniless and responsible for the care of his three children. In desperation, she appealed to his cousin, Knight Winthrop — and found herself irresistibly drawn to the witty, impossibly handsome confirmed bachelor.

NIGHT FIRE
75620-X/$5.99 US/$6.99 Can

Trapped in a loveless marriage, Arielle Leslie knew a life of shame and degradation. Even after the death of her brutal husband, she was unable to free herself from the shackles of humiliation. Only Burke Drummond's blazing love could save her...if she let it.